The Ghost of Squire House

Books by Joanne Pence
Published by Quail Hill Publishing

The Rebecca Mayfield Mysteries

SIX O'CLOCK SILENCE
FIVE O'CLOCK TWIST
FOUR O'CLOCK SIZZLE
THREE O'CLOCK SÉANCE
TWO O'CLOCK HEIST
ONE O'CLOCK HUSTLE
THE THIRTEENTH SANTA (Novella)

The Angie & Friends Food & Spirits Mysteries

MURDER BY DEVIL'S FOOD
COOK'S BIG DAY
ADD A PINCH OF MURDER
COOKING SPIRITS
COOK'S CURIOUS CHRISTMAS (A Fantasy EXTRA)

The Ancient Secrets Supernatural Suspense

ANCIENT ILLUSIONS
ANCIENT SHADOWS
ANCIENT ECHOES

Romances

DANCE WITH A GUNFIGHTER
THE DRAGON'S LADY
SEEMS LIKE OLD TIMES
THE GHOST OF SQUIRE HOUSE
DANGEROUS JOURNEY

The Ghost of Squire House

JOANNE PENCE

QUAIL HILL PUBLISHING

Quail Hill Publishing

PO Box 64

Eagle, ID 83616

Visit our website at www.quailhillpublishing.net

First Quail Hill Publishing E-book: September 2012

First Quail Hill Publishing Print Book: August 2013

Second Quail Hill Publishing Print Book: August 2018

ISBN: 978-1-949566-29-1

All houses wherein men have lived
  and died
Are haunted houses.   Through the
  open doors
The harmless phantoms on their
  errands glide,
With feet that make no sound upon the
  floors....

The stranger at my fireside cannot see
The forms I see, nor hear the sounds I
  hear;
He but perceives what is; while unto
  me
All that has been is visible and clear.

--Henry Wadsworth Longfellow
"Haunted Houses"

Chapter 1

JENNIFER BARRETT SHIVERED as she stared out the Greyhound window at the stark landscape of the northern California coast, at the crashing waves that mercilessly pounded boulders along the water's edge. The bus carried her away from San Francisco and all she had ever known. She hugged her coat closer and tried not to think about why she had left, or what she might find when she reached her destination. The bus wended its way along the steep precipices of the shoreline highway, the cold Pacific on the left and the rambling, moor-like vistas of the coast range on the right.

It was a bleak, hostile land, not at all as she had expected. She shut her eyes, pushing away the thought that she might have been mistaken, that her decision had been wrong.

It had begun with an ending: the death of her mother. Jennifer had always seen Rachel Barrett as being everything she wanted to be--attractive, poised and knowledgeable in the ways of the world. Next to Rachel, Jennifer had felt herself homely and awkward. Rachel was flashy in dress and demeanor, where Jennifer was quite the opposite. As long as she could remember she simply pulled her long hair back from her face in a rubber band or scrunchie, if not twisted and held in place with a large hair clip. She preferred sensible clothes that wouldn't look obsolete with changing fashions.

Her mother often accused her of melancholia, of being someone who looked at life without really living it. Rachel liked to say Jennifer's large blue eyes could be a good feature if she would only wear more make-up and learn too style her hair. And maybe look into paying for a little "help" for her thin, almost boyish figure. How the voluptuous Rachel had ever borne such a puny wallflower of a daughter was one of the things Rachel loved to chortle over to her friends, particularly when she thought Jennifer wasn't listening.

It was hard to believe that Rachel was now gone. She had been so alive, even at the end when she knew there was no hope for recovery, she had laughed in the face of death.

Then, suddenly, Jennifer found herself alone. Despite Rachel's story about a youthful marriage to Jennifer's father, who she said had been tragically killed, Jennifer had learned long ago that there was no "Mr. Barrett." She shuddered when she realized that Rachel might not even have been sure who Jennifer's father was. The result was that Jennifer was Rachel's sole beneficiary, inheritor of a small insurance policy and, amazingly, a property in Brynstol, California.

Jennifer stared at the attorney handling the estate in disbelief. "There must be a mistake. My mother never owned property!"

"No mistake. It was hers, and had been for some time," the attorney explained. "Rachel inherited it herself when she was about twenty, and seems to have kept it all these years."

"I can't believe it. I mean, my mother was not the sort of person to keep something as valuable as a house lying about. She would have sold it. I know she would have. Or, at least rented it. What's wrong with the place? It must be an old shack."

"Apparently not. From all reports, it's a sturdy

house."

He handed Jennifer the property description. The lot was approximately three acres, the house about 2000 square feet, two stories plus an attic. The house had been built in the 1880's and fell into the possession of relatives upon the untimely death of the original owner.

The lawyer continued, "Rachel once said something about trying to sell it after fixing it up a bit, but not being able to get her price. She had it boarded up, and apparently no one had entered the house for the past thirty-five years. Rachel did give me a name." He rummaged through his paper. "Ah, here. Gresham Innes. He's a realtor or something in Brynstol, and kept an eye on the place to be sure it wasn't vandalized. In any event, it seems the house has just stood there all these years. If you'd like to sell it, I'm sure he'll help you get a fair market price."

"I guess," Jennifer murmured.

"Gresham Innes can handle any sale, I'm sure. You won't even have to go up there."

She didn't speak for a long moment. "Where is Brynstol, Mr. Hartman?"

He gazed at her quizzically. "As near as I can tell, it's a small fishing village far up the coast past Cape Mendocino. It's quite an isolated area, well off the beaten path even for tourists. Apparently no one lives there except fishermen and dairy farmers."

She started. "The Mendocino coast?"

"That's right."

Barefoot she ran along the beach. The air was crisp, the wind blew fiercely, but she didn't stop. She was alone and crying, afraid, yet she ran...from someone or toward someone...she had no idea.

She struggled to ignore the image that flooded her mind. She hadn't thought of the dream, the nightmare, for years. It was one of those dreams that had recurred over and over when she was a child. When she told Rachel about it, Rachel just laughed and said to stop eating candy before going to bed.

Years later, as an adult, Jennifer remembered looking at a magazine with photos of the northern California coast around Mendocino, and found a beach exactly like the one in her dream.

--This picture looks familiar, Mom. Did we ever go there when I was little?

--Mendocino? Are you kidding me? Of course not! Bunch of superstitious cretins. I wouldn't waste my time.

So, as far as Jennifer knew, neither she nor Rachel had ever visited the area. And because of the nightmares, she hadn't wanted to. But now…why had Rachel lied to her?

Jennifer stood. "I am going to get a fair amount of cash from the insurance. If I had no rent to pay, I wonder if I'd be able to live on the interest from that money."

The attorney gave her an avuncular smile. "My dear, you'd be able to exist, but not much more. You couldn't be thinking of going to Brynstol, I hope. It would be lonely. A young, beautiful, single woman like you, coming into this money, you could really live it up! Have a ball here in San Francisco! Before you know it some man will sweep you off your feet and you'll have money to get your marriage off to a fine start. No, my dear, you couldn't possibly dream of leaving now!"

How many times had she heard words like

that, about the young man with that giant broom who was going to come along and "sweep her off her feet"? She had never found him and was, frankly, tired of looking. "I'll give it some thought," she told Hartman, and left the office, leaving him gaping in surprise at this unexpected reaction from his young client.

That evening Jennifer invited her best friend, Sue, to her apartment for dinner.

"I can't believe it!" Sue exclaimed after hearing Jennifer's news about the Brynstol house. "How exciting. Are you going to go see it?"

"I think," Jennifer said hesitantly, "I think I'm going to try living there."

"Living there?" Sue was incredulous. "I can see going for a vacation. Two weeks, even a month. But how can you think about moving somewhere you haven't ever seen? That's not like you at all! Even worse, how can you think of leaving the city? Leaving the Wharf, Chinatown, the Golden Gate Bridge? Your best friend?"

Jennifer smiled. "You don't make it easy, Sue! You're right, I'll miss you, and I do love this city. It's beautiful, but as I heard about Brynstol, I had a feeling--I can't really explain it--just a feeling that I should go there, be there." She shook her head. To say more could sound crazy. "For some reason, to go there to live, to make that commitment, feels right. Do you think I need a psychiatrist?"

Sue studied her. "You seem excited about this, Jen. I haven't seen you so enthusiastic about anything in a long time. Maybe, what with losing your mom and all, a change would be good for you. For a little while, at least. Just think, you can take up the violin again!"

"No, I'll never do that."

"Well, whatever," Sue said softly, but then brightened. "In any case, with the money you'll be getting, if you hate it there, you can always come back."

"Do you think?" Jennifer pressed her hands to her cheeks. "A part of me can't believe I'm giving this serious thought. My head tells me don't go, do as the attorney said, stay here, enjoy a little extra cash while it lasts. If I go with my gut-reaction though, I'll have to jump on a bus to Brynstol fast, before I chicken out."

"Then do it, Jen!" Sue clutched her arm. "If

you feel it's right, then try it, or you may always regret the not-knowing."

Chapter 2

IF, IN THE DAYS when he was alive, anyone had told Paul Squire he would spend eternity protecting a mediocre little house in an unpretentious community from a perpetual stream of pernicious relatives, he would have dismissed them as stark raving mad. They, however, would have had the last laugh, for there he sat, in the very same living room that he had built in his fleshier days, in sour anticipation of this latest progeny.

That he, who had always felt a wealth of familial pride, and bore the name of Squire to the point of arrogance, would have to witness what he considered the complete degeneracy of that family was Paul Squire's greatest burden.

He gave a long, deep sigh (or at least as weighty a sigh as one can give whose substance is in fact not much more than that which sighs are made of) as he thought back on the people who had already come to Squire House. He shut his eyes and shook his head. A thin hand reached up to rub his brow, to try to soothe the weariness of the years that so heavily weighed upon him.

He was of a rather delicate frame, just as he had been in life. It had been his wish that, having to return to the mortal coil as he did, he would have been allowed to return as handsome, well-apportioned and witty…but instead he came back to earth quite as he had left it: of haughty demeanor, a tall albeit slender build, and with a bent towards sarcasm rather than true wit. Of course, appearances hardly mattered to him these days. It was not as if he could have paraded good looks had he been given them.

Nevertheless, there were some things that no one should have to put up with, and a fusillade of ill-mannered relatives was one of them.

The first relatives arrived at Squire House seven years to the day after Paul Squire's disappearance in 1893. His actual death had never been accurately detected by the authorities. It had been a most peculiar death, which Paul presumed to be the reason for his present unnatural condition. His relatives simply noted the absence of Paul from Squire House and bided time until the seventh year when he was declared legally dead (a supposedly happier state an illegally dead, although to the party most intimately involved in the judicial pronouncement, it made no difference).

The first relatives to arrive were nothing short of dreadful.

They were from southern California, Los Angeles to be exact. Paul believed that that environment had transformed their noble heritage into such dull-witted boorishness as to make him doubt the validity of the relationship their birth certificates proclaimed.

The rowdy gaggle of southern Californians descended on Squire House in the year 1900. Paul was there, waiting to see them. He thought he could get rid of them easily. A few strange bumps in the night should cause even the most rational man to flee. But he did not count on such relatives as these. The main problem was that there were so many of them--two adults and six children. Any noises Paul made were dismissed by the adults as being made by the children and vice versa. Furniture moving, objects floating, all were laughed at and dismissed as a sibling or parent's clever trick.

Finally, out of sheer desperation, Paul resorted to a banal ruse which, would that he could, he would never admit to anyone. The merest thought of it years later caused him to shudder in embarrassment. After four days, Paul had been unable to make the slightest dent in the family's perception of the house as being anything less than absolutely normal. He realized stronger measures were needed when the children discovered Paul's paintings stored in the attic. He had been an artist, and although critics did not fall over themselves praising his work, Paul felt the paintings deserved better than having viscous little fingers pawing all over them. Therefore, that evening, as the entire family sat down to dine, Paul ran up to a bedroom, grabbed a sheet off one of the beds, threw it over his head and ran back downstairs yelling, *"Wooo, wooo,"* in his admittedly ghostly voice.

Pandemonium ensued. That, the otiose family finally understood. Of course, before they showed any fright, they first counted bodies to see which of them was missing and thereby know the perpetrator of the stunt. Eight bodies. Then they counted again. While all this counting was going on, Paul felt increasingly foolish flapping his sheet and caterwauling. Nevertheless, he persevered for he was a truly desperate man.

The family completed its second count, and had miraculously reached "eight" once more. Their more-blank-than-usual faces watched the sheet as it floated and swirled around the house, until, they jumped from their chairs, screamed and ran for the front door.

Five of the children and the mother cowered in the buckboard while the father and eldest son hitched the horses to it. They drove off to Brynstol, punctuating their flight with screams and moans.

The next day the father, bringing along for moral and muscular support five of Brynstol's biggest, strongest male citizens, returned to Squire House to collect the family's possessions. Prudently the still frightened former tenant waited outside. When the men finished gathering the clothes and such that belonged to the dispossessed clan, they then began to select other items that met their larcenous fancies. One man picked up a small chest, another a table in the living room and a third reached for a painting.

Paul was beside himself in fury and outrage at the audacity of these people. He knew he couldn't save everything and had to make a quick decision as to what was most valuable to him. There was really no choice: above all else his paintings must remain in Squire House. As a bruiser lifted the painting off the wall and gingerly carried it from the room, Paul took a firm hold of it and with a snap, snatched it out of the man's hands and rehung it.

The man stood with his mouth hanging open as the painting floated through the air and seemingly lifted itself onto the wall. The other men also froze in their tracks, jaws gaping, and eyes protruding with fear, amazement and utter astonishment. Paul was never sure which of them first found the ability to move, but suddenly one man darted for the door. This roused the others from their catatonia. All dropped whatever they were carrying and headed for the exit, their feet barely touching the flooring. They arrived at the doorway at the exact same moment, and since none saw fit to step aside and allow another to pass, they stuck there like too many pigs in a poke.

Never one to resist a little icing on the cake, Paul walked over to the dining room door near the front entrance. He swung the door open then shut, allowed the latch to click, then swung it open and shut again. At this, the men shrieked, their voices suddenly high and shrill as, using even more effort, they squeezed through the doorway.

Thus began the legend of the ghost of Squire House. People immediately reached the correct conclusion that it was Paul Squire guarding his house and keeping it as reclusive after his death as it had been during his life. Paul was gratified at their perspicacity, although for vanity's sake he hoped the story of the sheet didn't spread too far. He hated the idea of people thinking that his current state of existence was of such an unimaginative form.

Chapter 3

JENNIFER BEGAN PREPARATIONS to depart for Brynstol the day after her conversation with Sue. Her first action was to telephone Gresham Innes to tell him of her plans. She was initially alarmed at his reaction. The man sounded positively upset by the idea that she would come to Brynstol. Soon, however, he assured her nothing was wrong and declared he would have the house ready in about a month's time. Jennifer had plenty of time to notify her employer, an insurance company where she did clerical work, to get her inheritance in order, and to give up her apartment.

The weeks passed simultaneously fast and slow: slow as she anticipated going to Brynstol and seeing what it would bring, but fast as she thought of leaving San Francisco. Each cable car ride or walk in the fog-laden evening through the quiet old streets, became etched in her memory, something she wanted to carry with her always, no matter where she went.

Finally, this morning, the day came for her to leave the city. At six a.m., she found herself alone at the bus station, a solitary figure boarding her chariot to a new way of life with no idea of what she would find there.

Jennifer perked up as the bus passed through the town of Crespin's Cove, the town just before Brynstol. She wondered if it was a preview of Brynstol. No one got on the bus and not one of the eight passengers got off. Most of them were probably heading to Eureka, the only town of any real importance along the north coast. Fort Bragg, though popular for pleasure fishing, was a holdover from the past. The town of Mendocino gained importance almost solely from a minor tourist trade, and the small artists' colony found there.

Finally, the bus reached Brynstol. Jennifer was the only person to deboard. The bus "station" was no more than a sign over a bench in front of a general store. The main street appeared to be all of two blocks long. The buildings had old, turn-of-the-century wood fronts, but they were well-maintained, and painted in a way that emphasized their yester-year charm. The town had obviously worked hard to exhibit the facade it bore. Jennifer found it esthetically pleasing.

Carrying the one bag she had (the rest of her goods were being shipped), she made her way to Number 16 Main Street, a little one-story white building that must have been someone's home at one time. The names "Roundmore and Innes" were proudly displayed in gold lettering on the window, and below them the words--Realtors, Notaries Public, Financial Counselors, and Tax Preparers.

Jennifer strode up the two steps to the green front door, looked for a regular, electric doorbell, but instead found a chain. She pulled it and heard a bell clang.

In a few seconds an ancient little man opened the door. Rotund, with a fringe of white hair and apple red cheeks, he was dressed like an 1890's shopkeeper with baggy brown pants and a huge green vest over a white cotton shirt. Round, gold-rimmed glasses perched on the end of his nose completed the picture.

"You must be Jennifer Barrett," he said.

Jennifer's surprise quickly subsided as she realized in such a small town anyone else coming into this office would be known, a far cry from the way things were in San Francisco where she scarcely recognized her neighbors.

Jennifer said simply, "And you must be Mr. Innes."

"No, no, my dear." He patted his stomach. "I'm Mr. Roundmore, of course. Come in, come in. We were expecting you."

The room was cluttered floor to ceiling with papers, books and magazines of every shape and form along with three enormous desks, twice as many huge, comfortable looking chairs, and one small chesterfield. Buried in their midst was an older man as tall and willowy as the other was short and stout. He had a mass of snowy white hair and looked dapper in an expensive black suit.

"Well, well," said Innes, needing no introduction, "you did come after all. We were wondering. It's not often a young city girl decides to try staying up in these parts."

"Your town seems lovely," said Jennifer. "I hope to enjoy it here very much."

"Fine, fine! That's the right attitude!" Innes smiled warmly as he studied the woman before him. She had a surprising look of innocence for one who grew up in a big city. Innes noted that she was rather plainly dressed in a heavy, brown woolen suit, the type that would be referred to as "practical" while giving no indication of the femininity that the wearer might possess. Her hair, done in a hurried manner, showed she gave little thought to her features or looks. Yet, to the trained eye of Gresham Innes, a confirmed bachelor who had nonetheless made a lifetime of observing and appreciating women's looks, the fineness of Jennifer's features belied the plainness of her first impression. Her large blue eyes were especially captivating, clear and intelligent, yet with a hint of sadness. He felt his heart warm towards her as he wondered that she had never found the beauty she painfully hid.

Roundmore spoke, "We were wondering what you would be like. There's much curiosity about you already."

Such news took Jennifer by surprise and made uneasy. "Why should that be?" she asked.

Innes noted her reaction and spoke before Roundmore. "Just the usual curiosity about a new neighbor. You'll be left alone if you wish it, or you can have company if you desire that. Think nothing of it."

"Nothing of it," Roundmore chimed. "How about a cup of tea while you tell us about yourself!"

"Oh, well…" Jennifer turned towards Innes for help.

"I'm sure," Innes said, "Miss Barrett would like nothing more than to see her new home and have tea there, where she can relax."

Jennifer sighed in relief. "I'm looking forward to seeing the house," then added, "and I'm rather tired."

Innes took her arm and protectively whisked her to his car. He stopped at the local market so she could buy food and a few necessities. So laden, the two continued on.

Squire House stood only two miles from the town, a lengthy but doable walking distance to shops or whatever else Jennifer might need.

"We first removed the boards from the windows and doors," Innes said, "and I had a cleaning company remove the dust and sand from the house. It's astonishing how much dirt can accumulate even when a house is shut up tighter than a drum. You'll find it fresh and clean now."

"When did someone last live in it?" Jennifer asked.

"Years ago."

"Do you know who that was?"

"No. Sorry."

Those replies, Jennifer noted, were remarkably short for the long-winded Innes. "In any case, I do appreciate the help you've been to me," she said. "I suppose most people up here are from old families that have been in the area for years."

"That's mainly the case, but we do have some newcomers, and when the fishing is good that always brings in a few folks for a little while."

"Oh? How curious."

Innes looked puzzled by her words.

"I was surprised that my mother owned a house all these years, but kept it boarded up, neither selling nor renting it out. I expected that was because no one was interested in renting a house in this area, but now you state otherwise. It's very odd."

Innes nodded thoughtfully, then brightened a

bit and stated, "No mystery. Most of these renters only stay a season or two and then move on. A house has to be repaired stem to stern when they go. (Devilish people renters are.) Your mother, God rest her soul, did not want to be bothered with the constant turnover, repairs, and so on, that is involved in landlording, or landladying in this case (ha, ha) and she just said to close her up."

His answer didn't explain why Rachel didn't simply sell the house and party with the proceeds. Jennifer decided not to pursue the matter.

A half mile from Main Street the houses stopped; another half mile and the street became a narrow roadway with so many potholes it appeared the county's road repair department had forgotten about its existence.

The road zigzagged up the hillside, around boulders and groves of trees until, after one last curve, the vista opened. Perched regally in the distance, where the horizon and the crest of the hill merged, stood Squire House.

It stood over two stories tall, with a window-covered turret on one side and a porch spanning the front of the house. The varying shades of grays, tans, and white of its paint emphasized the gingerbread details of the Victorian design.

"Isn't it lovely?" Innes said.

Jennifer stared in silence. Yes, it was lovely, like something out of a dream. But then, unbidden and niggling in the back of her mind came the thought...*or a child's nightmare.*

Innes pulled into the driveway and stopped. Jennifer remained silent, unaware that in the house, a pair of frowning eyes observed the arrival of Innes' car with growing animosity.

o0o

Paul Squire glowered as Innes' beige sedan come to a stop on his property. *More relatives. How tedious.*

These onslaughts had gone on for nearly a century, one group after the other making their unwelcome way to his home.

After the first group of boors, ten years passed before the second gaggle of kin—four adults. Paul imagined that they hoped the "ghost" had disintegrated or had gone back to wherever ghosts come from. He showed them they were wrong and they left after the first night. A few others tried over the decades, and then he was spared any intrusion for nearly a quarter of a century until an attractive young woman named Rachel Barrett came to Brynstol. Although a descendent of Paul's, she did not even attempt to live in the house, but instead chose a lively inn on the coast where there were people, music and dancing every night.

He overheard her telling a youthful Gresham Innes that the ghost stories from Squire House's past were nothing but nonsense. She planned, however, to use them to increase the resale value of the house by making it more than just another old home. She had read somewhere that the most valuable castles in Europe all had ghosts in them, so why should California be any different?

Rachel hired some people to clean the house thoroughly and to repaint it inside and out. She spent her small savings on repairs and she even arranged for the installation of modern plumbing. Paul gave no trouble whatsoever to any of the workmen or, for that matter, to Rachel. He had always been a rather fastidious soul—in both existences—and thoroughly approved of this refurbishment. He had found the house's dilapidated state depressing, even for a specter.

When the work was completed, Rachel proudly put the house on the market. She left Paul's paintings and furnishings intact as she hoped to also sell the furniture. She used the paintings both to show that a true artist had lived there and to raise the price.

The first day the house was on sale a stream of people descended on it. Paul was beside himself. The last thing he wanted was to have hoards of strangers stomping through his residence, kicking the walls, jumping on the furniture and making witless, derogatory comments, "I thought it would be much more elegant!" "The color combination is dreadful—to think he was an artist!" and so on. The baleful tastes of the dread Philistines!

At first, Paul didn't quite know what to do, but then he realized that, all in all, it was best to do nothing and let the thrill seekers come and decide that Squire House was just a house like any other. He feared that if he took any action to scare them away, word would get out and cause even more people to come to experience a "haunting" first hand. Therefore, Paul hid in the attic with the bulk of his paintings, and barricaded the trap door opening with heavy trunks so that anyone who tried to enter the attic would assume the door was stuck.

There Paul sat, hour after hour, puffing on his pipe and glowering into the darkness wondering why he had been cursed with having such meddlesome people in his life, or, in his "existence" to be more precise.

By the third weekend, the number of curiosity seekers had dwindled and those viewing the house were interested in owning it. One prospective buyer had wanted to convert it into a restaurant...a greasy, malodorous one, no doubt.

Paul realized the need for circumspect ingenuity. He studied each potential buyer to see if any phobias were evident. A woman who was impressed by the openness and airiness of the house suddenly found herself shoved into a small bedroom closet whose door refused to open until she became quite hysterical. Another was chased around the house with a dead rat transported from the field. Some, with no clear phobias suffered general harassment.

Eventually, just as the curious had stopped

coming, so did those interested in a purchase. Rachel long before had left the area to return to San Francisco, leaving Gresham Innes in charge of the property. Innes never did see any of the strange experiences his shaken customers reported to him. He was at a loss to explain if they really happened or if people were letting their excitement-starved imaginations run wild. Being an eminently practical man, he convinced himself it was the latter. In fact, he developed a theory of mass hysteria based on his experiences with Squire House, and hoped to use it one day to launch a literary career.

Innes had also attempted to rent the house, but even at low rent he could find no dauntless takers. After relaying all of this bad news to Rachel Barrett, she told him to board-up the house and that one day she would return to see what she, personally, would do about ridding Squire House of its bad publicity.

Gresham Innes did as directed, but the beautiful Rachel Barrett never did return to Brynstol—much to Paul Squire's relief and Gresham Innes' dismay.

Then, three weeks ago Paul's thirty-five year reprieve was broken. Gresham Innes, who astonished the timeless Paul by how old he had become in just thirty-five years' time, came to Squire House with some workmen and landscapers. He had them remove the boards from the doors and windows, clean and paint the house inside and out, lay sod, and plant a flower garden. Innes told them he needed to make the home comfortable for Miss Barrett.

Paul could hardly believe his ears. At the mere thought of Rachel Barrett he gave a shudder. He remembered her as a queen bee with a hive of male drones surrounding her. Women like Rachel never paid any attention to Paul when he was alive. He found it ironic that even when dead she could come barreling into his home, completely disregarding his existence. All in all, it was mortifying.

And now the lovely Rachel was going to make a stab at Brynstol again after all. Paul steeled himself. If Old Maid Barrett wanted to clean up his house every thirty-five years she was quite welcome to do so, but she would never live in peace under his roof.

Over the month from the start of this latest round of cleaning until the date of Miss Barrett's scheduled arrival, the workmen finished their job. Even Paul was pleased by the state of the house. Nevertheless, as he sat waiting for his relative's arrival, his ethereal stomach began to churn in nervous anxiety at this latest disruption to his existence and his brows became increasingly crossed with vexation over the entire matter.

Now, the moment of truth had arrived.

Chapter 4

JENNIFER STEPPED OUT of the car. She had to agree with Innes that the house was esthetically pleasing, but something about it was cold. But why wouldn't it be after having been unlived in for over a century.

Still, it felt as if the house were glaring at her. She turned away from it and walked west, towards the ocean. At the edge of the lawn area, the land dropped away at a cliff, and far below was a narrow rocky beach. From this high point the ocean stretched so far she felt as if she should be able to see to China.

Innes joined her. "It's beautiful, isn't it?"

"Breathtaking."

"The house takes full advantage of the view as you can see." He turned and pointed to the many windows that faced the ocean..

She felt a chill. "It's almost as if it has eyes, watching everything before it."

Innes cleared his throat, "Ah, yes. Let's go

inside. These ocean breezes cut right through one's clothing."

Paul watched with amazement as he tried to figure out who this latest relative was. She clearly was not Rachel, the platinum-blond and voluptuous, for this relative had mousy-brown hair and was out and out skinny.

As Jennifer neared the house, Paul Squire got his first good look at her, then rubbed his eyes in disbelief. His expression became such that it seemed he were the one seeing a ghost. Fate was surely playing a trick on him and after all these years of having the faculties of a 40-year old man he was suddenly losing his mind and hallucinating.

How could it be that this person, whoever she was, so strongly resembled someone from his own past? Shaken, he decided he must study her, observe her up close. It was easy enough for Paul, due to his peculiar condition, to make himself scarce upon Jennifer's entry into the house.

Innes unlocked the door and Jennifer stepped into the entry hall.

To its left she saw a small dining room, a staircase just past it, and the kitchen appeared to be at the end of the hall. She turned right, into the surprisingly large living room, and stopped to stare at the beauty of it.

At one corner stood the round turreted area she had admired from the outside of the home. The windows gave a sweeping view of the ocean. A wall adjacent to that with the windows was made of stone and housed a large fireplace with a study wooden mantelpiece. Over it hung an oil painting of the ocean view from Squire House.

"The room is beautiful!" Jennifer cried. "And furnished! I never dreamed the place was furnished."

"Frankly, I wasn't sure what condition the furniture would be in, so I decided not to mention it. But then we found that with a good cleaning and a little polish, it was as good as new. Probably better." Innes nodded knowingly. "A lot of these are antiques. Fine antiques. Valuable pieces, or I should say in San Francisco they have value. Up here, to a lot of people they're simply old hand-me-downs. They'd probably rather have something new to boot, ha ha!"

By the time Innes finished, Jennifer had

wandered off to see the kitchen. The appliances were from the 1980's, but they had been as scrupulously cleaned as the rest of the house and they did seem to work, probably as adequately as when new.

"It's rather cold in here, isn't it?" Jennifer said.

Innes paled. "Uh, yes. I'll send someone up with wood for the fireplace. Out here, we only have electric heating, no gas pipes, and the electricity can be pricey."

"I'd like to see the upstairs," Jennifer said, as she headed towards the staircase.

"Go right head, my dear," Innes said. "I'll just stay at ground level, ha ha."

The master bedroom sat above the living room, and also had a turret and a fireplace.

Jennifer was relieved to see modern plumbing in the large bathroom, along with a claw foot tub and separate shower. There were two smaller bedrooms, one entirely empty and the other with only a couple of pieces of furniture.

"This will do quite nicely," Jennifer remarked when she returned downstairs. Innes stood in the hallway. "I'm stunned by the quality of this house."

"I'm so glad you like it." Innes added, "There's no telephone up here yet. The phone company hesitated to install all the cables and so forth since this place has been empty so long. But if you decide to stay, if you call them I'm sure they'll put a phone in for you, eventually."

"Is there cell service?" she asked.

"It's spotty in town, and I doubt there's any at all up here."

"I'm rather cut off, aren't I?"

"No need to worry. No one will bother you, believe me. And the way to town is certainly easy to find."

"That's true. I'll be all right. I'll get used to it I'm sure." Jennifer thought awhile then added, "Nevertheless, I think the first thing I'll do is get a dog. Maybe two. Big ones."

Innes laughed. "You'll become so accustomed to the quiet after a while you won't even hear it. You'll wonder how you ever survived in that city din." He looked around, his face suddenly wary. "Well, I do believe I should be heading back." He hesitated, as if about to say something more.

"Yes?" She asked, noticing his expression.

"What is it?"

"Nothing." He cleared his throat. "Nothing at all. I do wish you had a car—even a bicycle. That's all. I promise to look in on you early tomorrow morning. We can go down to Crespin's Cove, if you'd like. I'm sure you'll have a long list of things to buy."

As soon as Innes got into his car Jennifer shut the front door and turned back down the hallway to the living room. Now being alone she could study the house in a way she had felt somewhat inhibited about under Innes' scrutiny. She was particularly interested in the furnishings of the room. There was a gray and brown high-backed sofa, covered in thickly woven linen in a subdued tapestry-like pattern. The sofa stood in the middle of the room, facing the fireplace, with two large brown leather easy chairs on either side of it. On the opposite end of the room were smaller chairs and a table for card games and such or perhaps for serving dessert after dinner. In the turreted area, a window seat ran below the windows. On the seat were numerous pillows, each with its own style and interest, made out of silk, velvet or cotton, in muted interesting patterns. The entire room evoked a feeling of heavy textures, stability, and frank masculinity. Now clean and furnished as it was, it felt as if someone were already living here, someone who would come walking in at any moment and demand to know who this interloper moving into his house was.

Jennifer rubbed her arms as yet another chill rippled through her. It must be the damp of the ocean, she told herself, cutting through to the bone.

She put away her groceries and other purchases, and then made some coffee and a sandwich which she enjoyed sitting on the window seat. She could scarcely believe that she was really here, in her own house, in her own living room.

Refreshed, she carried her suitcase up to the second floor of the house. She decided that the former occupant was probably single, might possibly have been married, but definitely had no children since only the master bedroom showed any care in its furnishings. Jennifer would have immediately opted for a single inhabitant, except that the bed was large with heavy wooden posts and a high headboard. The pervasive masculinity of the living room was also felt in the bedroom, furnished with a highboy dresser and a low chest of drawers with a mirror over it. Jennifer observed that if a woman had lived here it would have also held a vanity.

The turreted area facing the ocean was bare, which surprised her.

She put away her belongings. She was glad that she had carried along her old "teddy" bear. She laid him on the pillow of the bed with great flourish and immediately felt a tiny bit more at home in his strange house.

Seeing her old bear on the pillow made her realize how tired she was. She had barely slept the night before so anxious was she about leaving San Francisco. Now, it was almost seven in the evening. The sun was on the edge of the horizon and would drop behind the ocean in a matter of minutes. She decided to lie down on the bed next to her old bear just long enough to watch the sun set and regain some energy before she went downstairs to prepare dinner. She was colder than ever, and seeing new sheets and covers on the bed, she kicked off her shoes and got under the blankets to try to warm up. She shut her eyes.

It seemed hardly any time had passed, yet when she opened her eyes again the room was pitch black. She awoke with a start, and took a moment to remember where she was. She knew she had been asleep, but for how long? She wondered what the time was, but knew she couldn't see the tiny hands of her wristwatch in such darkness.

What a fine fix, she thought. She remembered that there was a lamp on the bedside table. She should turn it on, but something caused her to hesitate to move, or to make any sign that she had awoken. She had the strangest sensation that she was not alone but that someone was watching her. How absurd, she told herself.

Yet she couldn't shake the feeling. She lay there with her eyes open, unmoving, listening. Moon and starlight gleamed through the window, and she saw in the corner a large, dark figure nearly six feet tall. Her heart nearly stopped from sheer fright, her breathing halted, as she stared at the object with all the intensity of her being.

The presence in the room grew more and more oppressive. She felt it as surely as she felt the warmth of the covers over her body in contrast with the iciness of the air against her face. She felt as if she would smother from the sheer weight of it and so, with a cry that she hardly recognized as her own voice, she groped for the lamp and switched on the light.

Chapter 5

SITTING UP IN bed, Jennifer remained absolutely still as her eyes took in everything in the room. Slowly she breathed a sigh of relief. She was alone.

How absolutely silly I am, she thought. To have allowed herself to get so frightened was new for her. She shook her head in disgust and went to the windows. The ocean looked serene in the moonlight, yet she could hear the waves pounding the shore and realized that the calmness of the water was but an illusion. She stood at the windows for some time, watching the sea.

"It is so beautiful here," she said out loud to nothing in particular. "Instead of enjoying this loveliness I scare myself about it! Such beauty to share with no one. That's the pity of it! It's a new life, Jennifer Barrett. Maybe, just maybe, it'll be a better one."

She spun around, fingers pressed against her lips. *I must be nuts. Not twenty-four hours in a house alone and I'm talking to myself!* She laughed aloud as she marched across the room to the dresser where she found her night clothes, changed into them, and got back into bed.

She did decide to leave the lamp on while she slept, however.

The next time she awoke, she was pleasantly surprised to find that it was seven a.m.

Noticing the lamp still lit in the morning light she chuckled about her nervousness the night before.

By eight-thirty she was dressed in jeans and a fisherman's knit sweater and downstairs drinking coffee after a breakfast of scrambled eggs and toast. The house seemed friendly today. And much warmer. To think that last night she had found the house cold and forbidding.

In less than an hour Innes arrived.

"How good of you to come so soon." She stood on the front porch. It was a lovely porch. She was going to have to get a bench or some rocking chairs to put out on it.

"Are you all right?" he asked somewhat hesitantly. "Everything okay up here last night?"

Jennifer was a little surprised by this question. "Why yes, of course. Why wouldn't it be? Won't you come in?"

Innes audibly sighed in relief at seeing her well.

Jennifer served coffee in the living room and Innes again asked about her feelings regarding the house. Pressed, she told him of her imagination in the middle of the night and how frightened she had caused herself to be.

Innes blanched. "It is an imposing old place, nothing more, ha, ha." His laugh sounded more nervous than cheerful.

He drove her into town where Jennifer telephoned Sue from the drug store and excitedly told her all about her new home. Sue could hardly wait to come up to see it. Jennifer's belongings were safely on their way north and should reach Brynstol that very afternoon. Jennifer was elated by that news. One of the items was a ten-speed bicycle, a foolish purchase for San Francisco, but it would be useful here, making it easy to ride to and from town so that she wouldn't need to impose on Mr. Innes.

Jennifer walked back to Roundmore and Innes' to tell Innes her belongings would be arriving that afternoon.

"Excellent! And, I have a surprise for you," he said.

"You do?" Jennifer was surprised already.

He smiled. "You mentioned something about wanting a dog for protection. You were serious, weren't you?"

"Yes," Jennifer said. "Don't tell me you know of a dog for sale?"

"As a matter of fact," he began, "a friend raises dogs up here. Sells them at a real good price, too. But you can make a deal with her. I already talked to her about you."

"Wonderful!"

Innes drove to the woman's home and as the car pulled up a terrific din of barks and low-wailing howls rose up.

No sooner had Jennifer and Innes gotten out of the car when three monstrous beasts that Jennifer was sure were bears, came bounding towards them. She jumped back in the car.

A stocky, squarely built woman, gray hair

flying akimbo with about two-thirds of it pulled straight up into a knot perched on the top of her head, appeared in the doorway of the house and bellowed, "Come back here!"

The three outside dogs and those back in the kennel continued to bark. "Shut up all of you!" she shouted at nothing and everything at once. As she marched towards them, Jennifer got out of the car. The dogs that were loose stopped barking and stood wagging stumpy tails. The others soon stopped barking as well.

"Sorry about the commotion!" the woman said in a voice as gravelly as the driveway they stood on. "You must be Jennifer Barrett." As she grasped Jennifer's hand in a vice-like handshake that reverberated through Jennifer's body, Innes introduced Gladys Petris.

"Pleased to meet you," Jennifer said as calmly as she could.

"Hey, Innes!" Mrs. Petris slapped Innes' back by way of greeting, nearly sending him flying.

She led the way to the kitchen to sit and talk, dogs included. It was obvious from the way the house was kept and its worn and fur-laden furniture that the dogs spent a good amount of time in the home making themselves comfortable.

"Do you know anything about these dogs?" Mrs. Petris asked Jennifer, pointing to her bearish three.

"I don't think I've ever seen that breed before," she said.

"Probably not." Mrs. Petris explained in her gruff way, as if it were too much of a bother to talk to anyone in complete sentences, "Called Bouvier des Flandres—bouvs for short. Good watchdogs. Loyal. Devoted to the family, not one-man dogs like Dobes and Shepherds. Don't need much exercise either. Won't run away. Affectionate to their family but stand-offish with strangers. Real powerful beasts. Have the most powerful jaws of any dog in the world—1500 pounds of pressure in one bite. Can take a man's leg off! Great dogs."

"That's a bit overwhelming," Jennifer murmured.

"Don't worry. They're not fighters, not aggressive at all, but they're brave. Defend only if and when they have to, and have the ability to defend if they need to."

"Well, that sounds like what I need living alone," Jennifer studied the odd beasts. They were big, large-boned dogs, as tall as German Shepherds, but dark gray, with thick, bristly hair that stood out over an inch from their bodies. Their ears were small flaps and their tails were two-inch puffs of fur.

By this time the dogs were standing around Jennifer and she was feeding them cookies and petting them. "They have beautiful brown eyes under that fur," Jennifer said.

"They're beauties all right!" Mrs. Petris said proudly. "Innes told me about you being up there alone, and you saying you wanted a dog and all, and I thought maybe we could help each other out. I run a breeding kennel here. I raise these dogs— real beauties in the breed—and sell them all over the country.

"I've got a couple of males that I don't want to sell because they've got qualities I want to breed for. But they're just kennel dogs here. By that I mean they spend most of their time out with the other dogs."

She looked Jennifer straight in the eye as she

got to the point. "Now if you'd like, you can borrow them, so to speak. They can live with you. All I ask is that when I want to use one for breeding that you'll bring him here for a couple of days. Other than that, as long as you live in Brynstol, they can be your dogs. That'll make them happier than being in a kennel. Bouvs are people dogs. They were bred to work for people, cow-herding, police work, guide dogs for the blind, you name it, and they're not really happy unless they've got a person to work for."

"Wow," Jennifer said, a little taken back by all this. "That's a great offer—but two dogs?"

"You'll need all the protection you can get up there!" exclaimed Mrs. Petris. Then, realizing what she said she tried to back off a bit. "I mean, not that it's dangerous as such or anything. Just lonely. A girl alone, like you—that's all I meant. Anyway," she cleared her throat, "it's these two." She introduced Beau, sixteen months old, and Jock, only eight months. Beau weighed ninety pounds, and Jock seventy. For the first time an almost motherly expression flashed across Mrs. Petris' hard-boiled, weather-beaten face. "They're young, so they'll soon think of your house as their house."

Jennifer and Mr. Innes just looked at each other. Jennifer's eyebrows rose in amazement and Innes looked uncomfortable.

Mrs. Petris gave Jennifer leashes, collars and enough food for a few weeks and sent her on her way with 160 pounds of canine in tow. Jennifer thanked heaven that the dogs were basically obedient had because if they decided not to be, she had no idea how she could handle them.

They filled the back seat of Innes' car and were terrifically excited about going for a ride. Despite being unable to see out of the rear-view mirror, Innes arrived safely back at his office.

"There's a little yard behind my office," Innes suggested. "What say we deposit them there this afternoon? I'll drive them to your place after the movers have gone."

Jennifer thanked him for everything. The afternoon was passing rapidly and Jennifer was beginning to worry about her belongings. At this rate she feared it would be dark before the trunk arrived. She walked up and down Main Street, checking out the shops. The Brynstol General Store was the heart of the community, and there was also a gas station, bank, feed store and doctor's office, not to mention Roundmore and Innes where everything legal, quasi-legal or paralegal needed in the community was handled.

Only a couple of women with small children were on the street. Both said hello to her, while studying her with unmasked curiosity. Everyone drove either a station wagon or a pick-up truck. The busiest place seemed to be the gas station, just off the highway.

"Finally," thought Jennifer as she saw an Eagle moving van turn off the highway. As it slowly meandered its way down Main Street, she jumped up and waved to the drivers to stop.

"Hi!" she said as the truck came to a halt beside her. "You are looking for Jennifer Barrett, aren't you? Number 10 Shore Drive?"

"We sure are, lady. That you?" A big blond fellow leaned out of the truck and smiled. He had on a tee-shirt with the sleeves rolled up to his shoulders, showing off tattoos on enormous biceps.

"That's right. Can I have a lift up to the house with you?"

"Sure, if you don't mind sitting on my lap!" The man laughed.

"No problem! I'll be right with you," Jennifer said, then burst into the law offices and told Innes the truck had finally arrived. They agreed that he would come up to Squire House around seven o'clock with the dogs.

Jennifer dashed back out to the truck. The blond fellow held the passenger door open.

"Hi again," he said smiling broadly. "My name's Oscar. That's Hans." He pointed to an equally large fellow sitting at the wheel. Jennifer greeted them both.

Oscar jumped in the cab of the truck first and patted his lap.

"I thought you were kidding." She laughed, but saw there wasn't enough room between the two men for anyone to sit, so, scrunching up in order not to bump her head, she somehow managed to fit sitting sideways between Oscar and the dashboard, with her arm around his muscular neck for support. They were off.

The two men joked and laughed, putting Jennifer at ease, and before they knew it they reached the front of the house.

oOo

Paul sat at an upstairs bedroom window as the truck pulled up. He slapped his forehead in exasperation.

"Good God! My sentiment in not scaring the baggage out of here last night is going to come back to haunt me yet!" Bending at the waist, nose to window, he scowled fiercely. "Look at that! An entire moving van, no less. How presumptuous! Has the baggage no sense at all? What if she hated it here? What if she were scared off her first night under my roof?!" He paced back and forth in front of the windows, growing more furious with each step. "What nerve! What gall! What perdition! Into my house she'll bring her mediocre, Woolworth specials without so much as a by-your-leave. Has the woman no shame? She must have no common sense, no practicality whatsoever. How did she manage to survive in a big city all those years? It frightens one to think of it!

"Frightens—oh, yes! How I could have frightened her last night if I so wished! But why exert myself? She did all the work based on her own too active imagination. If all my game had been so easy, I should never have had to work at all to keep this house rid of freeloading relatives!"

Fists on hips, he glared hard at the truck which had backed up to the front porch. "Look at the size of that truck! Once I do get rid of her I'm going to have to wait for movers to pack her rubbish out of here again. How very tiresome."

The passenger door of the truck opened and in a heap Jennifer and Oscar spilled out of the truck onto the driveway, both laughing so hard they could barely stand up again.

"How despicable!" Paul snarled. "She cavorts with hired help. Never before have I been cursed with such a relative!"

Jennifer and Oscar walked up to the front door of the house and Jennifer took out the key. Just as she was about to open the door Oscar took hold of the door knob. "Allow me," he said, pushing the door open only to be struck by a frigid blast of air.

"Thank you," Jennifer said.

"My pleasure, Miss Barrett."

"My pleasure," Paul mimicked. "Oaf!"

"It's cold in here," Oscar said, rubbing his

hands together. "Worse than a walk-in freezer."

"Isn't it though?" said Jennifer. "It was quite pleasant this morning. How strange." She wandered through the downstairs to see if a window had been left open. But no open window was found, and besides, it was warm outside.

Hans carried in the first few boxes. "Where do you want these?'

"I marked all the boxes." She checked the label. "Okay, these are for the kitchen. Right back there." She pointed down the hall.

"Sure is cold in here," Hans said.

Jennifer stood puzzling over the temperature as Oscar approached the door carrying more boxes. She smiled and started toward him when his feet flew out behind him and rose up so high he practically did a headstand before he came back down to earth, face first. The boxes scattered. Jennifer gasped, then ran to him to see if he was hurt.

"Who tripped me?" he bellowed as he jumped up, fists raised, and spun around searching for his attacker. He was unhurt, but livid. Hans stood in the doorway of the kitchen looking confused. Oscar slowly realized that no one else was there. He shook his head.

"I swear, it felt like someone tripped me," he repeated, turning in a slow circle and rubbing his forehead. "That's the strangest thing. I guess I just lost my footing."

"Are you okay?" Jennifer asked. "Do you want to sit?"

"No, no, I'm fine. I hope these boxes are."

"Of course he's fine," Paul muttered, arms folded as he leaned against the front door frame. "He landed on his head, didn't he?"

"Let's see," Jennifer inspected the boxes. "These are all bedroom and bath linens and such. No harm done. The bedrooms and bathroom are upstairs. Just one bathroom—it's a very old house. I guess I should be grateful it's indoors!"

"Let me take that," Hans interjected. "No stairs for you," he said to Oscar, "until we're sure you are all right."

"Okay. Who am I to say?" Oscar continued to rub his head as he headed back to the truck.

Quickly the two men unloaded the truck. Jennifer had shipped all the furniture and belongings from her small three-room apartment. She had them load the second and third bedrooms with the furniture until she decided what to do with it. Looking at the difference between the quality of her furniture and that already in the house, hers was most likely destined for Goodwill.

When they had finished unloading the truck, Jennifer invited them to stay for a bite to eat.

Hans replied, "Well, we don't have much time. We need to head north another eighty miles, but a sandwich wouldn't damage our schedule."

The men sat at the kitchen table as she quickly prepared ham and cheese sandwiches. They turned down her offer of wine, but took some coffee. Jennifer, hungry, joined them.

"This is sure a pretty house, Miss Barrett," Oscar said. "Mighty cold, but pretty none the less."

"Thank you," said Jennifer. "It wasn't so cold yesterday, or this morning. I guess I'll have to keep the fireplace going a lot."

"Do you mind if sometime when I'm up this way I stop by?" Oscar asked, hope shining in his eyes.

Jennifer was taken aback, but he seemed to be

a nice guy. She smiled. "Not at all. I would like that."

Oscar's smile was so wide, she noticed one cheek formed a dimple. Maybe he wasn't so bad looking after all.

Hans stood up. "Well, since you two took care of that bit of business, we should get going."

"Give me a minute—the call of nature," Oscar said.

Oscar went up the steps and Jennifer and Hans talked, waited, and talked some more, quietly wondering what was taking Oscar so long. And still they waited. Finally, they heard banging and Oscar's calls.

They ran upstairs. Jennifer reached the bathroom door first, paused for a second, then turned the knob and pushed the door open. Oscar stared in disbelief from the open door to Jennifer to the open door again, then his brows crossed in anger. "How did you do that?" he demanded.

"Do what?" Jennifer asked. "Are you all right?"

His face turned five shades of purple, and his tattoos practically glowed in an even deeper shade.

"I'm all right! It's this house that's not. That door was stuck. I pulled with all my might and I couldn't get it to open. The knob turned. It unlatched, but it stuck. I even took the hinges off and still couldn't get it open." He jutted out his palm with the two hinges on it.

Jennifer gawked at the hinges, then at the door she had just opened. "You mean there are no..." She hadn't finished her sentence when the door started to slide off the hinge brackets on the door jamb, away from the wall and heading towards the floor. It landed with a resounding "thwack."

They stood silently a moment looking at the door at their feet. Jennifer mewled, "But it opened very easily..."

Oscar and Hans silently picked up the door and put the hinges back on.

Jennifer tried to apologize but Oscar continued to give her harsh looks. As the men took their leave, she was quite certain Oscar would never return.

She went outdoors and gathered some firewood Innes had had delivered. Along with old newspapers from her packing she was able to get a healthy fire going which did helped warm the air.

About seven-thirty, Innes arrived with the dogs.

Beau and Jock behaved well on the leashes, neither pulling nor straying, but walking with dignity towards the house...until they reached the doorway. They stopped short. The fur on the backs of their necks stood straight up. Innes stepped into the house ahead of them and tried pulling them in, and got nowhere. Beau crouched down and began howling. Jock, the baby of the two, rolled over on his back and cried. Innes looked ready to cry himself in exasperation at not being able to get the dogs to go into the house.

Jennifer came upon this din while struggling to carry a twenty-five pound sack of dog food into the house. "What in the world?" she asked.

"They won't go inside."

"This is too heavy for me to stand here and argue with them. I'll be right back," Jennifer said as she stepped over Jock and went off to the pantry with the dog food.

She came back to the doorway in time to witness a tug-of-war between Innes and Beau.

Innes was losing and was on the verge of being pulled back outside. This was too much for Jennifer.

"What's going on with you two?" she demanded of the dogs. Beau and Jock stood still and looked at her. "I don't know what you think you're doing, but this is my home and your home. Do you understand? It may be weird and it may be cold, but right now it's the only home you or I have. So you may as well get used to it. Come! Now!"

She took the leashes from Innes, and gave them a tug. The dogs took a couple of steps forward. "That's good boys. Come on," Jennifer coaxed. The dogs stepped through the doorway and were in the house.

"Finally," said Innes, breathing a sigh of relief as he shut the front door behind them. He began mopping his brow with his handkerchief.

As soon as Jennifer took the leashes off the dogs, like a shot they both ran barking into the living room. Jennifer and Innes followed right behind them.

Once in the room, however, the dogs stopped

barking and looked around confused. Then, they ran up to the large overstuffed leather chair near the fireplace that also had a view of the ocean. They sniffed furiously all over it, on the seat, back, legs, sides, making little whimpering noises as they did.

"What are they doing?" asked Jennifer. "What scent are they finding on that chair?"

Innes looked pale as a ghost. "Oh, why, um," he stumbled, "perhaps the people who cleaned here left something on the chair. Some cleaning fluid, perhaps?"

"I guess that's it," Jennifer said, thoughtfully. "Would you like some coffee or tea?"

"Tea sounds fine. Any traditional flavor," Innes said. As Jennifer went to the kitchen, he sat on the sofa and watched the leather chair. "You may have met your match this time!" he chuckled aloud to no one in particular.

The dogs finally stopped sniffing the chair, went over near Innes and lay down.

Innes helped Jennifer set up her stereo and unpack some CDs. After discovering they both liked classical music, they listened to Bach as they quietly talked by the light of the fireplace. Before he left, Innes accompanied Jennifer as she walked the dogs, then made her promise to lock the house up tight after he left.

Jennifer had enjoyed her first guest in her new home, her first evening as a hostess.

"Beau and Jock," she said, and the dogs, which had been cozily asleep by the fire, looked up at her, "I'm going to spoil you two mercilessly, so we may as well start now. Come on. You can sleep in the bedroom."

At that she shut down the first floor of the house, led the dogs up to the bedroom and went to bed. This night held none of the terrors of the previous night for Jennifer. She had a fire going in her fireplace, the dogs were with her, her radio was turned low to an all-night station. She curled up, warm and comfortable in her bed, and slept.

Paul Squire entered the bedroom and looked at her sleeping so cozily. As a gentleman, he had never taken advantage of his ethereal position to abuse the privacy of any visitors to his house, especially not a female visitor.

He noted how different the room seemed with her in it. Before bed, she had bathed, and the scents of her bath salts and shampoo permeated the upper floor of the house. A floral perfume lingered now in the bedroom, with the fire and the softly playing classical music. None of his former visitors had been classical music lovers, as he was. To listen to it all through the night seemed almost magical.

He sat in an easy chair she had brought from San Francisco. It was yellow and blue, a French country pattern, and mercilessly feminine, yet it was comfortable and fit perfectly in the room. It would be rather cruel, he decided, to rouse her this evening. She had had a busy day and seemed quite exhausted. He would let her sleep and perhaps tomorrow start his campaign to ride Squire House of the abominable woman's presence.

She turned over in the bed, and he realized as much as he liked sitting there, it wasn't the right thing to do. For this night at least, it was her bedroom, not his. As he left, he patted Jock and Beau's broad heads. The dogs, in turn, wagged their stumpy little tails and didn't seem bothered by him in the least. Paul had always been fond of dogs. A pity, he thought, that the dogs would have to leave when he frightened Jennifer off his property.

Chapter 6

FINALLY, THE DAY arrived for Sue's visit. Nearly three weeks had passed since Jennifer last saw her friend in San Francisco. Sue was taking off work that Friday morning to drive straight up the coast to Brynstol.

Jennifer went down to Roundmore and Innes' about two o'clock to wait for her arrival, absolutely elated at the chance to see her again.

Jennifer had met several of her neighbors who were uniformly surprised at her staying at "Squire House" as they called it. They explained to Jennifer that the original owner was an eccentric artist named Paul Squire. No one would come right out and tell Jennifer why her staying alone in the house perplexed them, but it was obvious that it did, and whenever she questioned Innes, he claimed to know nothing about the house's history.

In general, people kept to themselves in Brynstol. This suited Jennifer nicely. She had always suspected that she was a loner, but in San Francisco there were always people nearby—her mother, Sue, co-workers, or simply masses of strangers. All that had changed and Jennifer was finally able to find out what it was like to truly be alone. She liked it, and no one here seemed to find her weird for feeling that way.

"There she is!" Jennifer shouted to Innes as she stood looking out the window of his office. Innes looked up from his interminable pile of papers with a start, yet caught only the most fleeting glimpse of Jennifer as she dashed out of the office.

Sue had parked a little blue Miata, and stood beside it looking bewildered as Jennifer approached. She was tall, with short blond hair that curled and wisped around her face in the breeze. The two friends embraced.

"What's with this car?" Jennifer exclaimed. "I didn't know you were getting a new car! It's beautiful!"

"It's not mine. Not with my rotten salary. And I haven't robbed a bank since you saw me last." Sue smiled. "It's my new boyfriend's car. He let me borrow it. His name is Brent Cooper, and he's simply dreamy!"

"Dreamy, no less?" Jennifer had to laugh at Sue's high school expression. "I do look forward to hearing all about him."

"Oh you will, believe me."

Sue could hardly get over the change in Jennifer. The lines of tension and pallid terseness that were so familiar were gone from her face, replaced by a light tan, a blush of pink on her cheeks, and a look of well-rested contentment. Instead of the tight knot she so often pulled her hair into, it flowed freely and softly down her back, nearly to her waist, gleaming and shining in the sunlight. She's beautiful, Sue thought, amazed at the discovery.

They got into the Miata. The sun was low in the horizon, glowing magnificently behind Squire House as they reached the top of the hill, making it look large, imposing and beautiful. Sue was awe struck. "I can't believe it," she cried. "It's absolutely marvelous!"

Jennifer was pleased beyond words at Sue's reaction. "Wait until you see the inside."

As they pulled onto the driveway Beau and

Jock came running towards the car, barking furiously. Sue slammed on the brakes. "Are they dogs or barking bears?"

"Pussycats, really." Jennifer turned to the dogs and told them to be silent. They obeyed. "They're great companions, and they keep away strangers," added Jennifer.

"Don't let me be the first to tell you," said Sue, "but those monsters will keep away friends too! Especially this one!"

"Don't worry. They're fine. They even sleep in the bedroom with me," Jennifer added.

"I won't waste my breath asking about your sex life."

When the two went indoors Sue was as enthusiastic about the house as Jennifer had hoped she would be. In preparation for her visit, Jennifer had readied one of the smaller bedrooms for use as a guest room, using the bed and some of the furniture she had brought from San Francisco, mixed with a few Squire House antiques. The result was an attractive old-world style room. Sue fell in love with it.

Jennifer cooked a simple dinner and they ate at

the little table in the living room. The sun had just set completely, leaving the sky a dusky, reddish-grey. A fire blazed in the fireplace.

"I've never used the dining room yet," Jennifer confessed. "I enjoy eating in this room and watch the ocean's ever-changing views."

"Why didn't you tell me what a fabulous place this is?" Sue exclaimed. "I had visions of some old dump! But it's got such atmosphere!"

"It surely does," Jennifer agreed.

Sue continued wistfully, "What stories this place must have to tell! Don't you wonder sometime, what it could say if it could talk? I wonder if anything really exciting went on here."

"I've never heard anything."

"But something must have happened here," Sue insisted. "I mean a house like this just doesn't sit around year after year collecting dust for no reason at all. You know what I mean? I wonder how we can find out what that was."

"What do you mean, 'we'?" asked Jennifer. "I may not want to know. What if it's something terrible? I'm the one who'll have to stay here alone, you know. I don't even want to talk about it."

"Oh come on now, don't be silly! What do you know about the place? Anything?" Sue asked.

"Just what some neighbors said."

"Tell me!" Sue was all ears.

"The original owner was an artist. He lived alone and never married. After he died they hunted for some relatives. The closest they could find were some distant cousins in San Francisco. My great-grandfather was one of them. When he died the house passed to my Grandpa Lawrence, then to my mother and now I have it. That's all I've heard. It might all be gossip. Not very exciting is it?"

"Did any of them ever live here?"

"Apparently not, although my mother did visit it and hired Gresham Innes to take care of it. I have no idea why she didn't sell it, take the money and run."

"Maybe because it's so lovely?" Sue suggested.

"Come on, the loveliest thing in the world to my mother was the green of US dollars. I really don't understand that part of the story. Perhaps my grandfather forbade my mother to sell it, but no such restriction was in her will. Besides, I don't think she ever obeyed anything else he told her to do. As far as I'm concerned, why she kept it is the biggest mystery about this house," Jennifer concluded.

"What about the painter? Is he known at all? Is his work any good?"

"That's his painting over the mantle. There's another in the dining room, and one in the master bedroom. More are apparently up in the attic."

"There's an attic here too?" Sue was growing more curious about the house. "I've always dreamed of exploring an attic in an old house. Who knows what we'll find up there. How exciting! Can we go up there now?"

"No way." Jennifer was horrified at the thought. "I'm sure it's dark and filthy."

"Tomorrow, then?"

"Perhaps. But we've got plenty of time."

"You don't really want to see what's in that attic, do you?" Sue asked.

Jennifer looked puzzled at first, then she nodded. "You're right. I don't. I still don't feel very much at home. Everything was in place when I arrived, and it looked so much like someone else was living here, it seemed I didn't belong--as if the house itself wanted me to leave. Eventually, as I displayed my own possessions that feeling lessened. But to go through the belongings of the former owner, to handle them, laugh over them, whatever, seems wrong. Perhaps I'm being silly. I am curious, I'll admit that. "

Sue didn't reply; she knew what was coming.

"Maybe with you here," Jennifer continued, "I'll be able to look at the stuff."

"Yes!" Sue shouted with glee. "I knew you'd say that."

oOo

The next morning Sue slept until nine-thirty, remarking that she couldn't believe how quiet and peaceful the house was.

After a light breakfast, they packed a picnic basket and headed out to explore the countryside and the beach.

Driving along the winding country roads in Sue's little sports car was fun. Jennifer pointed out the few places of interest she knew. One of her chief pleasures, however, was to finally see the houses where some of the people she had met in town lived. Most were small, single-story homes that often were in need of repair. She realized how fine her house must seem to the people of this town, which made it all the more mysterious that the house had been boarded up.

The two women found an open field off the roadway, parked the car and walked into the brush until they reached a grove of pines providing shelter from the warm sun. They sat to enjoy their picnic.

"Well, Sue," said Jennifer, her sandwich half gone, "Tell me about Brent. When did you meet him? What's he like?"

"Where to start?" Sue grinned. "Soon after you left I was feeling really depressed. I felt my life was the pits, you know? So finally I said what the heck and decided to go back to that creepy singles bar we went to a couple months back. You remember that place?"

"How could I forget! We walked in, turned around and ran out again."

"Like I said, I was really low. I went in, sat down and bought myself a drink. A really obnoxious guy came along. I told him to flake off. He decided I was playing hard to get, the creep! I was miserable and trying to get rid of him when I heard this deep, masculine voice say, 'My sister asked you to leave. I suggest you listen to her.'

"I turned around, and saw Mr. Dream standing beside me. A mouthful of sparkling white teeth like some movie star. And a tan like someone who can sit in the sun all day oozing cocoa butter. 'Hello, brother,' I said, all the time I'm thinking, what's this gorgeous hunk doing talking to me? He's like a movie star, I swear. Sandy blond hair carefully styled, no barber shop for him. Blue eyes, flashy dresser. I figured he's talking to the Queen of the Frizzies because he looks so pretty by comparison. Maybe that way he could pick up some really neat woman or something. But he stayed with me."

"He sounds perfect!"

"He is. I've seen him each weekend since, and a couple of times in the middle of the week. And he told me I could drive his car up here this weekend since mine is such a clunker."

"Are you in love with him?" asked Jennifer.

"What girl wouldn't be?"

"What's he like? What does he do for a living?" Jennifer inquired.

"He's a weatherman on TV. The local morning show on KPIX. He works a few hours and makes scads of money. He sails, skis, jogs, has a fantastic apartment, he's intelligent, and has his lifestyle figured out."

"Are you sure he's for real? He doesn't have a hidden wife, or ten?"

Sue laughed. "I know. He's hard for me to believe and I know him well. Very well," she added with a wink.

Jennifer joined Sue's laughter.

After lunch they felt it was time to move on. They drove to the beach to take advantage of one of the few fogless days in an area almost perpetually caliginous.

The beach Jennifer chose was difficult to find as it lay hidden from Highway One by some high boulders that looked about to drop straight into the ocean, but at the base of the boulders, there was a small, sandy area.

The access to the beach was by fire trails that meandered slowly but not too steeply along the hillside.

The women parked the car at the top of the hill

took a footpath to the beach.

"The scenery is absolutely beautiful here," Sue said. "Everything is so rugged. The very air seems charged with the full force of nature, as if we're small and insignificant and all this is eternal. It's humbling, and should put our petty trials into perspective."

"This land makes you poetic, Sue."

"It's my philosophical side coming out. My God, Brent should hear me now. He'd never believe it."

"Does Brent know 'Sue-the-philosopher' or 'Sue-the-depressed' yet?"

"Hell no! 'Sue-of-the-million-laughs' is his girl!"

"I see," Jennifer said, becoming increasingly concerned about this too-perfect-to-be-believed relationship. Sue was a person who lived life exuberantly, her highs and enthusiasms were great fun, but she could become equally low and depressed.

Jennifer noticed a young man climbing over some rocks near the water. "Someone's out there," she said.

They spread their blankets on the sand and watched him scramble over more rocks until he reached the beach. Then he ambled along the water's edge towards them.

"Hello there," he shouted. "I thought I was the only one who knew about this beach."

"Are you saying this beach isn't big enough for the both of us?" Sue said.

"No way! You can share my beach any day!" He had a nice smile, and his black eyes sparkled mischievously. His hair was the color of those eyes, and although he was not overly tall, he seemed very strong, as if his work involved some sort of physical labor.

"Your beach!" Jennifer and Sue said almost in unison with mock indignation.

"Okay, okay, point taken," the man said. "It's a beautiful day, don't you think?"

"What do you think, Jennifer?" Sue asked in a stage whisper. "Should we talk to him?"

"We can chance it," Jennifer responded with a smile.

Sue lifted her gaze to the stranger. "It is very nice weather. My name is Susan."

Jennifer chimed in. "Jennifer Barrett."

He nodded. "Good to meet you, ladies. I'm Ross Alderworth from Clevewick."

"Won't you join us Mr. Alderworth from Clevewick?" Sue said, holding out a chilled Diet Coke.

"Thanks." He popped the top, and then looked inquisitively at Jennifer, "Aren't you the woman living in the old Squire House?"

"The one and only."

"Is she famous around here?" Sue asked.

"You had better believe she is!" he said. "No one has been able to live in that house since I've been alive, I know that."

"'*Able* to'?" Sue looked at Jennifer who shrugged in surprise. "What do you mean?"

"Well you know!" he said, then saw the expectant looks on the women's faces. "You don't know?" They shook their heads. He thought for a moment, then said simply, "Everyone says the place is haunted."

"Haunted!" Jennifer and Sue exclaimed.

"How incredible!" Sue laughed. "Is that why no one has lived there all those years?"

"So they say," said Ross. "I don't know too much about it, though, it was all pretty long ago."

"Who's supposed to be haunting the house?" Jennifer asked. No laughter was on her face, her eyes intense.

"They say it's the original owner, Paul Squire." Jennifer gasped.

"God, how weird!" Sue exclaimed.

"Why would he do such a thing?" Jennifer asked, her voice scarcely above a whisper.

"Word is, he had a love affair that went bad. Anyway, he lived up there all alone and he painted. Nice paintings, too, I hear. Then one day he disappeared. Never a trace. The folks around here left the house as he last had it, waiting for his return. Eventually, he was declared dead and some relatives got the place, but everyone who tried to live there soon ran off swearing the house was haunted. No one could keep it rented, and couldn't sell it either. Not until you." He gave her a look filled with curiosity.

"I guess that goes to show the effect stories have on people's imagination," Sue said. "Since we hadn't heard such stories, nothing seemed 'spooky' to us. We find the house beautiful and charming. I guess if we had heard such drivel we would have been afraid there too, right Jennifer?"

Jennifer was lost in deep thought. Hearing her name, she started. "Oh." A pause. "Yes, right, that's right. So that's what's behind it. Paul Squire."

"Do you know anything about him, Jennifer," Ross asked.

"No, nothing at all, really. Although, it is strange, but living in his house, with his furniture and his books, I almost do feel that I know the man. His character, anyway."

Sue shuddered. "Don't talk like that! You'll make me believe those ghost stories if you do!"

Ross spoke, "Have you seen his paintings, Jennifer?"

"Only the three hanging in the house."

"But there are more," Sue said, her eyes glistening with excitement. "In the attic. We haven't seen those yet."

"Why not?" he asked.

"Simple enough," Jennifer explained. "The door is overhead, flush with the ceiling, and the one time I became curious and tried to open it I couldn't. It's too heavy. I could get the door to budge a little, but then I didn't have the strength in my arms or shoulders to push it open while trying to keep my balance on the ladder. I plan to ask a workman to open it for me next time I call one there for some other reason."

"Now for the truth," Sue said, "which is Jen doesn't want to go through the dead man's belongings."

"That's not the only reason," Jennifer said indignantly.

"The man's been dead at least a century," Sue said. "Everything is yours now."

"Legally perhaps," Jennifer mused.

"I'd love to get into that attic!" said Sue.

"It would be interesting," Ross agreed, meeting her gaze.

"In any case, the door doesn't open. It's stuck," Jennifer added.

"I'll unstick it for you," Ross said, "whenever you're ready, that is, to go into your own attic." He glanced at Sue and winked.

Jennifer threw up her hands. "I give up! I know you're both right. It's silly of me to hesitate to see what's in there."

"Better do it soon before she changes her mind," Sue said to Ross.

Ross thought a moment. "I've got to work tomorrow until late afternoon, but other than that..."

"How about tomorrow night then?" Sue eagerly suggested.

It was agreed upon. Jennifer and Sue rose to leave the beach, and Ross walked with them up to their car. He had parked his pickup not too far away, so they took their leave.

"God, he's so good-looking and nice!" Sue said.

"Oh?"

"Don't even try to pretend you didn't notice! No wonder you like it up here. All these handsome Daniel Boone types running around in the woods! How fantastic."

"Believe me," Jennifer said, "up until today, Mr. Innes was the only single man I've met in this entire area; and I can't see him blazing a trail through tall weeds."

"Ross Alderworth from Clevewick," repeated Sue. "What's Clevewick?"

"It's a big dairy ranch, not too far from here."

"Does Ross own it?"

"I don't know who the owners are. The Clevewick family, I suppose. I never heard of any Alderworths. Anyway he said he had to work tomorrow—remember? He must be one of the hired hands there. They employ a lot of people. How you do romanticize, Sue!"

"Me! Ever hear of the pot calling the kettle black?"

Back at Squire House, they spent a quiet evening talking about old friends and old times.

Sue was the first to retire upstairs and Jennifer found herself alone in the living room. She enjoyed the sound of the waves softly lapping the rocks along the shore.

She rose from her chair and walked across the room to the bookcase, still filled with the belongings of the original owner. Opening the glass doors, she looked over the books. Many were classics, and many she had never heard of. Most were histories or biographies. They gave her a sense of the man who chose them.

She chose one, Milton's *Paradise Lost*. The

cover groaned perceptibly as she opened it. Inside she found a nameplate stating "This is the Property of …" and then in a large flourish Paul Squire had signed his name. She slowly traced the signature with the tip of her finger, then closed the book and put in back in its long held spot on the shelf.

She shut the glass doors and stood, wondering how many more books, paintings and other belongings the next day would bring to light.

She gazed a long time at the painting above the mantle. "Paul Squire," she whispered, then turned away, locked up the house, and went to bed.

Chapter 7

AS SOON AS JENNIFER shut the door to her room, Paul went to the bookcase and reached for the book she had held in her hand. He opened it and looked at the flyleaf. What would make her study his signature in that way? He expected that people in the town had spoken of him to her, most likely weaving strange tales about which they knew nothing. Could such stories be affecting her in some mysterious way? He could tell by her taste in music and books that Jennifer was a romantic. Her literature was overwhelmingly slanted towards the nineteenth century romantics—the Brontës, Dickens, Eliot; and her music was heavy with Rachmaninoff, Brahms, Schumann and Tchaikovsky.

Oddly, her taste greatly matched his. He sat in his favorite chair and lit his pipe, book on his lap.

Whatever was she doing tonight? What had caused her to stare at his books so? He took several puffs on his pipe as he pondered these questions.

Finally, he shook his head at his foolish reaction to the skinny baggage. Why should he care what she thought? If only he had gotten rid of her he would have been spared such anxieties! That one iota of his incorporeal self was concerned about how she felt troubled him.

He must make Jennifer leave Squire House…although he did have to admit that, generally speaking, it was rather pleasant having her there. She was actually an intelligent, sensitive woman—a species Paul thought did not exist. The image of her out in the world, alone, was strangely distasteful.

He took the book and flung it back into the bookcase, where it landed sideways on the shelf. Paul didn't notice this, however, because he had, at the same time, shut the bookcase's door and hurled himself back into his chair. He sat and brooded over the situation the rest of the night.

Chapter 8

JENNIFER AND SUE spent the next afternoon with Mrs. Petris, where Sue was given the entire history of the Bouvier des Flandres, and a pretty complete course in dog husbandry. Beau and Jock went along for the visit and Mrs. Petris could not have been happier about their progress. Jennifer had been giving them both obedience lessons, and they were not only well-behaved but clearly devoted to her. Mrs. Petris confessed that she had been a little worried about Beau—she was afraid he had spent too much time as a masterless kennel dog to ever be of much use in the house. But he seemed genuinely pleased to be rid of his carefree kennel days and to have the job of watching over Jennifer. He worked hard at trying to prevent her from getting lost, being hurt by strangers, or getting into one of the myriad entanglements human creatures seem so prone to. Jennifer was pleased to report that he took his job seriously and that she felt exceedingly safe when he was around.

Back at Squire House they spent the rest of the day exploring the nearby land with Beau and Jock. They found some footpaths and old trails. Most paths seemed to abruptly end in the middle of nowhere, but the women enjoyed climbing around nonetheless, as did the dogs.

The one place Jennifer made sure to avoid was the beach at the foot of the cliff near Squire House. When Sue suggested they climb down to it, Jennifer said she had been told the cliff was too steep and dangerous. Sue looked a bit dubious, but didn't push it.

As the sun sank in the western sky, the two returned to the house, ate a simple supper, and waited for Ross Alderworth.

While Jennifer sat on the window seat her eye noticed something strange about the large bookcase with the glass doors. She couldn't quite figure out what it was so she crossed the room to study the bookshelves more carefully.

"What in the..." The book that she had been looking at the previous night, the one with Paul Squire's signature, was lying on its side instead of being upright on the shelf.

Sue looked up. "What's wrong?" she asked.

"Did you look at any books here?" Jennifer inquired.

"No. Why?" was the response.

Jennifer decided to shrug it off. "Oh, I guess one of the dogs knocked this book over. I thought you might have been looking at it and could give me a quick critique. Nothing special."

Sue laughed, "I guess you'll have to ask Beau for the book review—Jock is probably too young to read yet. Or..." She began to sing the "*do-dat-do-do, do-dat-do-do*" theme from *The Twilight Zone.*

"Very funny!" Jennifer forced herself to laugh. She picked up the book to place it correctly on the shelf, then stopped and lifted it near to her face. She fanned the pages with her thumb, smelling the distinctive scent of pipe tobacco. Since Jennifer was not a smoker she was very sensitive to that particular odor. She hadn't noticed it on the book the day before, although she had noticed it on a few occasions in the living room, especially near the large leather chair.

"What is it?" Sue asked.

"I love the smell of old books," Jennifer said,

then hurried back to the window seat and sat, trying to rationalize the irrational.

oOo

Paul Squire could have kicked himself for being so careless with that book. Jennifer puzzled him, flipping through the pages. He wondered what caused her to do that. Could she suspect anything? That was impossible. He had been quite circumspect. Scarcely more than a fly on the wall. He pushed the thought from his mind to replace it with wondering who Ross Alderworth was and why he was coming to Squire House.

Paul knew something was up, but he didn't know what it was. He decided he had better observe the situation carefully. After all, Sue was just a temporary guest—the type of disruption in his household with which he could live. Ross Alderworth, however, was a neighbor. If he and Jennifer became friendly he might start showing up at all hours of the day and night. Were that to happen, Paul vowed Jennifer would be out of Squire House so soon it would make her head spin.

And so it ended up, unbeknownst to Ross, that there were in fact three people awaiting his arrival that evening.

oOo

The sun had set completely. The moon was new, so it was quite dark outdoors, and only a few stars could be seen in the fog-tinged night sky. The women were beginning to wonder if Ross forgot about them.

"Maybe he had to work tonight," Sue said, disappointment heavy in her voice.

At that moment, both dogs jumped up from their places on the living room rug and ran to the front door barking with excitement.

"Sorry I'm so late," Ross said as he entered. "Had a problem with one of the dairy cows."

"That's okay. It's not late for us," Jennifer said, quieting the dogs.

"Hey, a couple of the Petris' bouviers. They're great dogs, aren't they?" He bent down and patted them both. "We've got a few that herd cattle for us. They do a fine job."

"They're wonderful," Jennifer agreed as she took Ross' coat.

He stood in the hallway and looked around. "So this is the big haunted house. I never dreamed

I'd be in here. It seems pretty nice, actually."

Paul glowered more than usual seeing the handsome young man in his home. He found use of the word 'haunted' to be in decidedly bad taste.

"Pretty nice!" Sue said, she'd been waiting in the living room, but joined the others. Ross's face lit up when he saw her. "Wait until you see the living room!"

"Good to see *you* again, Sue," Ross said following her.

"Wow!" he exclaimed as he tore his gaze from Sue to peruse the room. "No wonder you like it here."

He walked across the room to the big leather chair by the fireplace. Jennifer started. "Don't sit there!" she cried out. "This chair," she pointed to its mate on the opposite side of the fireplace. "It's much better."

Ross did as told.

She knows! Paul thought. *But how? I couldn't have given myself away.* Then, relieving the blame from himself, he considered that it might be some extraordinary sensitivity or power of observation on the part of this newcomer.

Sue was also surprised by Jennifer's outburst. "Why better?" she asked.

"Oh, well," Jennifer thought quickly, "one of the legs is weak. I need to get it fixed. Anyway, would you like some refreshments, Ross? I've got beer, wine, coffee, tea?"

"A beer sounds good," he replied.

He hardly took two or three sips of it when he said, "Well, ladies, I'm ready anytime you are."

"Oh good!" Sue jumped to her feet.

It was the moment Jennifer had thought of with increasing dread, and now here it was, a reality. "Okay, the attic is this way." She stood, feeling like a condemned man on his final walk.

The attic! Paul jumped up from the leather chair and took a step forward not even looking where he was going. He bumped into the ashtray stand that had been placed alongside the chair and it toppled over.

Sue nearly jumped out of her skin. "What happened?" she cried.

Ross lost all the coloring in his face.

Only Jennifer managed to control her feelings and appear somewhat composed. "Oh, it does that all the time. It's top-heavy. Old furniture throughout the house. I should have warned you." Quickly she headed up the stairs to the attic.

Paul wondered what steps he should take as he followed them up to the attic.

On the second floor, Jennifer took a ladder from the spare bedroom. "There's the attic door," she said pointing towards the ceiling.

"No problem." Ross positioned the ladder under the opening and began to climb. "This ladder's not as steady as it looks," he said as the ladder wobbled and swayed under his weight.

"Be careful!" cried Sue.

"I guess the ladder is old like everything else in this house," Jennifer said with a nervous chuckle.

"Present company excepted," added Sue.

Ross pushed the attic door trying to determine which direction it should open in. "I think I know how it's supposed to open, but it feels like it's stuck or something. Actually it feels like there's something on top of the door holding it shut, but that's impossible unless you've got awfully large rats up there that can shove furniture around."

"Rats!" Sue shuddered. "Maybe we should forget about this, I don't want to see any giant rats get disturbed and decide to come downstairs for a visit."

Suddenly all of Jennifer's hesitation about going into the attic evaporated. "Try Ross, you'll make it. I want to see Paul Squire's paintings more than anything else in the world!"

"Don't give up girls!" Ross said. "I'll get this sucker yet!"

At that he began to push harder on the door. Suddenly it not only became "unstuck," but flew open with ease, swung all the way over, and landed with a loud *thwack*.

"Wow, didn't know my own strength," Ross muttered.

Ross climbed higher on the ladder and boosted himself into the dark attic opening. "Do you know if there's electricity up here, Jennifer?"

"I doubt it! Just a second." She ran downstairs.

Sue called up to Ross, "How does it look?"

"I can't tell. It's pitch black. There seems to be a lot of stuff. It's cold, too, really cold. I can't imagine why it's so icy. It's like a meat freezer."

"Do you think there are any rats?" she asked.

"If there are, they're frozen solid. What stuff! My eyes are getting a little accustomed to all this, it looks a little incredible."

"Why? Wait, here comes Jennifer," Sue said.

Jennifer came up the stairs carrying a large kerosene lamp. "I keep this in the pantry in case the electricity ever goes out. This should give us enough light to see what's up."

"Who's coming up first?" Ross asked.

"You go on," Sue told Jennifer. "It's your attic."

"Okay." Jennifer handed the lamp to Ross, then climbed the ladder. As soon as she was high enough to see into the attic she stopped. Sheets covered everything.

"Pretty ghostly isn't it?" Jennifer said to Ross.

Sue yelled up to them, "Don't mention that word!"

"I'll help you up." Ross steadied Jennifer as she climbed the rest of the way into the attic.

Sue was right on her heels and rapidly scrambled through the opening.

Ross slowly pivoted with the kerosene lamp so

that the entire attic was cast in light for a time. The peaked roof of the house caused the ceiling to slope on two sides.

The three stood rooted to the spots where they first stepped into the attic.

"Cold, isn't it?" said Jennifer.

"Yes, we commented on it while you were downstairs," said Sue.

They looked around the room.

"Well," said Ross, "here we are."

"Yes," said the two women in unison.

"I guess we ought to do what we came for," Jennifer said.

"Where do we start?" Sue asked.

"Start by being careful you don't fall down the attic opening," warned Ross.

"Right," Sue said nervously. "No wild parties or running around."

Ross and Sue looked at Jennifer. She spoke, "Well, how about that sheet right there? Shall we remove it and see what's under it?"

The three looked at a large square but flat object, covered by a once-white sheet. It was most probably a painting.

"That looks good," Ross agreed. "Who should do the handiwork of removing the cover?"

"You do it, Ross," Jennifer said.

"Me? No, I think it should be one of you ladies."

"Please," Jennifer said. "I'll hold the lantern."

Ross nodded, then handed Jennifer the lantern and slowly took several small steps towards the object she had pointed out as the first to be unveiled.

Sue shuffled a couple of steps sideways to get a better view.

Jennifer raised the lantern high.

"Are we ready?" Ross asked.

"Ready or not," Jennifer said, "let's see it."

This is what Paul Squire had dreaded about the three coming into the attic—strangers observing his work. He had received no recognition for his art when alive. People had found his painting technique peculiar. No eyes but his had looked at these paintings for over a century. The same anxiety he used to feel as a young man taking work to a gallery rushed back at him. Having his paintings here, now, was a clear statement on the reaction they received from gallery owners.

"Okay," Ross said. He reached behind the object to find the ends of the sheet. Having found them he slowly lifted the sheet up the back, raised it up over the top of the object, and then flung it aside in one fell swoop.

Jennifer took two quick, small steps forward, placing the lantern in a way to get a better look.

It was a scene near Brynstol showing two fishermen standing on a windy, foggy beach. One had just caught a fish and was removing the hook from it, and the other fisherman looked like he was gathering up his fish and his gear in order to pack up to go home. The remarkable thing about the picture was that the men were so alive. There was movement and intensity in it. The men were working—real and natural, yet it was not a still-life type picture, nor in any way like a photograph. It was obviously influenced by the impressionists of the time, although more in the spirit of Manet's work than of the more famous Monet.

"How incredible!" Sue cried.

"I think I like it," Ross murmured.

"It's a fascinating study," Sue commented.

"How real they look, like they should get up and walk right off that canvas! Don't you like it Jennifer?"

Paul looked at Jennifer's face with apprehension.

Jennifer studied the painting further before replying. "He is a marvelous painter. He really has talent."

Paul, inaudibly, sighed with relief and pleasure.

"Yes, he does...um, did—didn't he?" Sue agreed. "What a shame this painting has been buried up here."

"Perhaps he was ahead of his age?" Ross asked.

"Probably so," answered Jennifer. "Painting has progressed so rapidly that the impressionists seem tame these days. But a hundred-twenty or so years ago, in California, it's no wonder the paintings are in an old attic instead of on display somewhere. It's a shame, isn't it?"

"I guess so," said Sue, "but then, how many people want dead fish in their living room?"

Ross joined Sue in her laughter but both

stopped short as they saw Jennifer did not share their humor.

"Well," said Ross, "do we want to see another?"

"Yes," said Jennifer, "that one." She pointed to another sheet covering something that looked like it would be a painting.

Paul found that the unveiling of his painting shook him to the core, as if they were dissecting his soul. He knew he should go back to the living room to recuperate, but he couldn't bring himself to leave.

Ross removed the second sheet with the same flourish as he had the first, and sure enough there was another painting. The style was similar to the first, and was of Brynstol's main street. Many buildings looked surprisingly similar to ones still standing.

This painting lacked the remarkable impact of the first, simply because it was a much more traditional subject matter. The technical ability was nevertheless quite evident.

"Let's see what's under here," said Ross, removing a blanket that covered some rectangular objects. Under the blanket were two wooden trunks, one atop the other.

"I wonder if they're unlocked?" said Sue.

"Jennifer, do you want to do the honors?" asked Ross.

"I'll try," Jennifer replied. She handed Ross the lantern as she searched for the clasp on the top trunk. There was no lock so she lifted the lid.

Linens. It was nothing but a trunk full of sheets and towels.

"Now why would so many of these be stored up here?" Ross asked.

Jennifer studied them a while. "They are fine material, and appear to be unused. I wonder why not."

The two lifted down the top trunk to see the one beneath it.

The second trunk was somewhat more interesting than the first. They found a pair of curtains that looked like they would have belonged in a bedroom at one time, also table cloths, napkins and two aprons. At the very bottom of the trunk was a set of sterling silver. Ross lifted the lantern higher as Jennifer held up a spoon to better see the design on it.

Suddenly, Sue cried out and jumped back from the sheet she had begun to lift to see the painting it covered.

"What's wrong?" Ross asked.

"Sue, you're white as a ghost!" Jennifer crossed the small attic towards her friend.

"I...I," Sue stammered, then took a deep breath. "It was just the light, I'm sure. A painting, back there. It startled me, but I'm sure it was just my imagination. The light is bad here, you know, that's all. Sorry to have been so silly. Let's go back to looking at the trunk."

"Oh, no," Ross said. "I've got to see what was so scary."

"It was nothing, really," she replied.

"Nothing? Quite a reaction for nothing. Let's see it," Ross urged.

Ross bent over and picked up a small canvas, letting the covering slide to the floor.

"I don't believe it!"

"What is it?" Jennifer asked. Ross slowly turned the painting towards her. It was a portrait of a young woman, dressed in nineteenth century finery. The background was the sea-green of the ocean, and the wind blew against the woman's loosely flowing cream-colored gown.

Jennifer couldn't believe her eyes. Somehow she managed to control her voice as she, with false calm said to Sue, "I see what frightened you. The face is remarkably similar to mine." In the portrait she saw herself as she might have looked were she of that earlier age, with her hair in curls framing her face, and large, blue eyes smiling with a joy of life and self-assuredness that Jennifer had never known. The woman was beautiful and elegant, and the painting had clearly been made with a loving hand. In that moment, Jennifer envied the woman who seemed to be a far better, far happier version of her.

The three of them stood as if transfixed. The portrait, like the others, bore Paul Squire's signature, and looked equally old, yet Jennifer could have posed for it yesterday.

Jennifer was the first to speak, "Do you two mind if we go downstairs now? I think I've had enough of old attics for a while."

"Sure, let's go," Sue and Ross agreed.

Ross steadied the ladder as the women climbed down it.

"Please leave the door open, Ross," Jennifer said. "I may want to go up there again soon to get some of those pictures to hang in the house."

"Good idea," Ross said. "They deserve to be seen. Call on me if you need any help."

Jennifer thanked him as they entered the living room. Silently and thoughtfully she went to the kitchen to make a fresh pot of coffee.

"That was wild!" Sue whispered to Ross as they stood at the windows overlooking the ocean. "I thought I'd die when I saw that picture. It's the spitting image of Jennifer. I don't understand it at all. I thought I'd fall away dead!"

"I thought you would too! You were completely shaken."

"As if you weren't?" Sue said with a smirk.

"True," he admitted.

A chill caught Sue and she rubbed her arms. "This is a strange house. The former owner's presence is still so strong in it. Do you feel it, Ross?"

"I suspect what we're feeling is a result of

having rummaged around in his things all night."

"I guess that's it," Sue said. "But I do worry a bit about Jennifer being here alone."

"Alone? Won't you be staying?" Ross had not understood how brief Sue's visit was to be.

"Tomorrow I leave for home."

"So soon!" Ross exclaimed. "When will you be back?"

"I'm not sure. This is a long way from San Francisco," Sue replied.

"Just a few hours," he said.

"Six? Or more? At least I'm glad Jennifer has you for a friend now," Sue told Ross, "so I won't feel she's completely alone here."

"Oh, that she's not. There are plenty of people nearby who know she's here by herself and keep an eye out for her, even though she's not aware of them."

"That's good news!" Sue was surprised to hear this.

"That's what folks are like in a small community like this. We're fishermen and ranchers. Independent, yet we know there are times we need each other. When that happens, we help each other out. Yet each must carry his own weight, too."

"It sounds ideal."

"I wouldn't go that far," Ross said, "but it is a nice place to live."

"What's a nice place to live?" Jennifer asked as she entered the room carrying the coffee and some cookies.

"Ross was telling me that this town is," Sue explained. "I would agree."

The three continued to talk about Brynstol, studiously avoiding mentioning the attic or its contents.

Sue told Ross a bit about her home and job in San Francisco. The three enjoyed each other's company and talked long into the night.

Finally Ross realized it was time for him to leave. He promised to return to see Jennifer before long, and made Sue promise to return to Brynstol soon.

Sue and Jennifer retired soon after Ross left, as Sue had a long drive ahead of her the next morning.

Chapter 9

JENNIFER WAVED GOODBYE as Sue drove down the hillside, watching until the little blue sports car disappeared on the winding road. Beau and Jock seemed to sense Jennifer's sadness and hovered close beside her. She patted their heads, and they accompanied her back to the house.

She puttered around until everything was back in the same order as prior to Sue's visit. Sue was a let-it-fall-where-it-may person while Jennifer was a place-for-everything-and-everything-in-its-place type. By deciding to never try to be roommates they remained friends for over a dozen years.

Whenever Jennifer passed the attic opening, she was tempted to go up and root around in the trunks and boxes, and to look at more of Paul Squire's paintings. She successfully avoided giving into those feelings until she finished straightening up. Then she went into the bedroom and convinced herself that it was, all in all, quite foolish not to go up into her own attic to look at everything she had inherited.

The longer she lay on the bed the more she thought about the attic. Finally, she could stand it no longer, went to the ladder and climbed up.

She relit the kerosene lamp that had been left beside the opening. There were twelve paintings in total—the fishermen, the street scene, the woman who so resembled her, several ocean scenes with small boats and fishermen, one scene of a crowd of people at a fair, a still-life of wildflowers, and a couple of city scenes. She also found a number of sketch books and spent the afternoon going through them.

Jennifer decided the paintings should be displayed. All except the one that made her uneasy. Upon closer inspection, there were differences in their looks, and the face had been done with the skill of an impressionist, so it was more an *impression* of Jennifer than a photo-like image. Still, she couldn't deny what must be a family resemblance.

She took the fishermen painting downstairs to see how it looked in sunlight. To get the large canvas down the ladder was awkward to say the least.

In the sunlight of the second floor, once out of the false kerosene glow of the attic, she was able to appreciate the subtleties of light and dark color in the picture, and the textures created with the brush strokes beyond the richness the colors themselves employed.

It was a painting worthy of a place of honor, and Jennifer carried it to the living room with a good idea of the exact spot she wanted it hung. But as soon as she stepped into the room, she came to an abrupt halt. The picture began to slide from her hands before she tightened her grasp.

Sitting calmly and comfortably in the large leather chair by the fireplace was a man, a mature man, not young, but hovering towards middle-age. He had wavy hair, a cross between light-brown and dark blond. His face was thin with a high forehead, a rather long nose, and pale gray eyes. He wore an old-fashioned, woolen hounds-tooth jacket in soft heather and wheat colors over a loose muslin shirt, baggy dark brown trousers, and brown slip-on shoes. A column of smoke that billowed from his pipe carried the tobacco smell Jennifer recognized.

He leaned back in the chair, studying her as carefully as she studied him.

The most amazing thing of all to her was that Beau and Jock were lying at the man's feet as if he were their oldest friend in the world.

"So you decided that oil should be in this room. I agree." His voice was calm and smooth. "I'm quite fond of it, myself."

Jennifer's heart was pounding with fear and sheer astonishment, and at the same time, she was frozen to the spot. "Who are you? What are you doing in my house?"

"Whose house?" he asked with a twitch of the corners of his mouth and an arch lift of his brows. When she made no reply he said, "Come, come, my good woman. You know who I am."

"I have a good idea of who you are dressed up to make me think you are! How stupid do you think I am?" Jennifer replied hotly, feeling frightened and angry at the same time, wondering if she were the brunt of a practical joke, but not knowing what to do if she were not. "Whoever you are, I think you should leave my house right now or I'll call the police."

"Call? Really?" He smirked.

Jennifer stiffened. She had no phone up here, and no way to get help.

"Oh, relax! You're perfectly safe." He was clearly irritated. This was not the reaction Paul Squire expected when he decided to speak with her. "My dear young woman," he said, walking to the mantelpiece and propping an elbow on it as he took another puff of the pipe, "for what possible reason would I wish to perpetrate a ruse of any type upon the likes of you? In fact I could care less about anything you do or say—though you have shown some degree of tastefulness in your expressions over the paintings. I am who I am and I see no reason for you not to accept such a fact. As for *you* ordering *me* out of here, don't you have that backwards?"

She drew in a quavering breath and raised her chin. He was taller than she expected, and quite slender. He looked down at her with a smirk. "Are you some other relative of Paul Squire's? Do you think this should be your house?"

"Balderdash!" He waved his pipe with a flourish, punctuating his words with it. "I'm finding I was incorrect in my assessment of you. I thought you were more perceptive, but I see you are as ignorant as all others of your sex!" He tamped down the tobacco. "I'm surprised to say I actually feel a slight disappointment at this discovery."

He put the pipe in his mouth, taking another draw as he walked to the turreted windows and looked out at the ocean. She studied a noble profile with a high straight nose, pronounced cheekbones, and a pale, sensitive mouth. The way he had turned his back on her she felt dismissed as unworthy, which both angered and saddened her.

Beau rose up and walked over to where the man stood, then sat beside him looking up with adoring devotion. The man patted the dog's head and continued to ignore Jennifer.

She remained silent until she could bear it no longer.

"You are not Paul Squire!" she shouted.

"Oh?" He didn't face her.

After another silence Jennifer stamped her foot, something she hadn't done since she was a teenager. "Paul Squire would be over 150 years old!"

He stiffened. "Or?"

"Or?" she repeated his word. Her breathing came fast before she whispered the only logical response to his question. "Or dead."

"How perspicacious." He nonchalantly continued to stare out the window.

Jennifer grew furious. "Get out of my house! I don't know who you are, or how you've gotten in here often enough to make friends with my dogs but you won't be friends with me! You must think I'm the biggest idiot in the world to be insinuating what you are. If this is some sort of a con-artist game, it won't work. I give you one minute to leave and never return or I will get help to force you from my house. What kind of a loathsome creature are you, coming here like this?"

As the man turned and looked at her, the sad disappointment in his gray eyes belied the venom on his tongue. "You are right!" His voice was soft and thoughtful. Somehow that made his words ring true to her. "I should have known better. For some reason I thought you were different from the others that have come here all these years. The avaricious, cultureless oafs that would have stripped Squire House to the bone and then gone on their bleating, low-brow way."

Their gazes met as he continued. "Perhaps it was because of your remarkable resemblance to *her* that I suffered you to stay, or perhaps it was because of that first night here, you were frightened and alone, yet so determined to make this house your home, it caused me a grudging admiration." Then he shrugged and a small smile touched his lips. "Of course, I soon saw that your taste in men is abysmal."

"Whatever are you—"

His look grew arch. "That Neanderthal whose only value in life was that he could juggle heavy furniture had the audacity to think he would be welcome in this house as a visitor! And you would have allowed it?" He strode towards the doorway. "I was quite sure it was only some sick thought that you should have people around that caused you to make him feel the door would ever be open to him. I decided you would in fact thank me, in the long run, for taking an action to assure that the moron would never return. I was pleased at how easily it worked."

Jennifer was speechless at this outburst of arrogance, but startled that he had seen so much of what had occurred with Oscar the moving man.

He paced back and forth, arms folded. "I suppose I should be frank and admit it was not just for your sake I got rid of him. I know his type. Get him around a woman and he'd pant and slobber until the two ended up rolling about in bed. Quite frankly, such a scene would have been revolting to me beyond all endurance. I really had to spare myself."

She saw red. "What nerve!" she shrieked—and Jennifer Barrett had never before shrieked in her life—but this man was intolerable.

Making his voice louder, Paul continued, "But then, you became rather pleasant. You were doing a fine job making Squire House your home. I did approve. Even your giddy friend Sue was somewhat acceptable. That man Ross was not, but that could have been easily taken care of."

Jennifer had to sit. Her legs could no longer support her.

He stopped pacing as he added more tobacco

to his pipe and lighting it. After a few puffs, when he spoke again, his voice was much calmer. "I most admired you when you spoke of the paintings. You showed insight and feeling that I doubted a woman could possess. A kindred spirit, I surmised, someone to speak to after all these years. And so after, I assure you, much soul-searching and great trepidation, I decided to attempt to meet you and speak to you—to share the intellectual bond that I had thought we possessed."

Then he stepped towards her, his eyes cold. She shrank back against the sofa. "But instead what do I discover? That you are no different at the core than all other women! Vile creature! You rebuff me in such a manner and cannot see beyond the end of the nose on your face. Women are nothing but materialistic, conceptual idiots, two-faced, unfeeling, unthinking, heartless boors. I am sorry I ever deigned to offer you my company."

At that he turned and strode from the living room.

"How dare you speak to me that way!" Jennifer cried after his receding figure. She sat absolutely still, waiting to hear the front door slam shut. She did not. On jelly-like legs she ran to the hallway. It was empty. Her anger vanished as she walked down the hall to the kitchen. No one was there. She crossed the hall to the dining room. It too was empty. Could he have gone upstairs without her hearing the steps? She could not imagine it. The stairs were so old that the slightest weight on them caused loud creaking noises.

She tip-toed back to the living room, still listening for some sound to tell her where this mysterious man had gone.

Shaken, she sat in a chair and felt herself shuddering from the frigid blast that suddenly filled the air. Her mind kept racing back to the words the stranger had spoken. How did he know all those things? Had he actually been hiding in the house? That was impossible. It was a small wood frame building. The walls were thin. It was not the sort of home in which one found secret rooms and passageways.

So how did he know? How did he booby-trap Oscar-the moving-man into the bathroom without being seen? Although, she had to admit, she was just as glad to never see him again.

What did this all mean? She went into the pantry where she kept a hammer and found some materials for picture hanging, and put the fishermen painting on the living room wall. It was bold, realistic, yet impressionistic. A painting of life on the ocean in a home beside the ocean.

She made herself some coffee and as she sat with it, she wondered if she had fallen asleep and dreamed all of this. Perhaps she was a victim of narcolepsy, or in the throes of a strange illness? She began debating which was the worse fate—narcolepsy or having a strange man…a strange and disarmingly good-looking man despite his bad temper…lurking around the house.

As she debated this, however, her eye caught something that settled the argument. She rose from her chair and walked over to the mantelpiece. There, atop it, lay a smoldering pipe.

Chapter 10

THE WEEKS PASSED slowly and uneventfully. Mr. Roundmore gave Jennifer books and guidance on gardening and with his help she planted several vegetables. The garden soon blossomed into full productivity, which allowed Jennifer the convenience of living on very little money. She bought chickens for eggs, a goat for milk, and baked her own breads and desserts. In that way, only occasional purchases of meat, fruit, nuts and condiments, covered the majority of her food needs.

The frugality with which she was able to live meant that she only spent a small amount of the interest she received from her own savings and her mother's insurance policy. She expected to eventually need to find some means of livelihood, but at least the wolf wasn't at the door.

Beau and Jock ate quite a bit, but Mrs. Petris let Jennifer buy dog food from her at kennel bulk prices which made their kibble relatively inexpensive. Jennifer had grown quite attached to the dogs and would not have given them up no matter how costly their upkeep was. They had become, effectively, her best friends in Brynstol and with them she shared all her innermost thoughts and dreams. She brought them everywhere with her. The community became accustomed to seeing the solitary woman riding slowly on her bicycle with the two big gray bear-like dogs lumbering along beside her.

Her biggest expense was a satellite dish for television reception, computer access, and even wireless texting since there was no cellular, cable, DSL or anything else remotely reflecting the twenty-first century in the community.

She had made a number of acquaintances in Brynstol but Gresham Innes was her most faithful companion. He often came to Squire House for dinner or just to pass a pleasant evening talking to Jennifer.

Ross visited as well a couple of times after Sue left. But the two were not as comfortable together as they had been when Sue was with them, and the visits were short and somewhat awkward.

A telephone was installed after a four month wait. She talked to Sue a few times, but generally they sent emails. Sue was still seeing Brent Cooper. He had been "into" body-building for a while, and bought all kinds of weight-lifting equipment. He and Sue joined an expensive health club where all the best people were said to work out. Then he decided he wanted to learn scuba-diving and bought lots of diving gear, as did Sue. They hadn't used any of it yet because the northern Pacific was difficult and cold for novices, so they were planning a trip to Mexico. The last time Jennifer heard from Sue, Mexico was out and India was in because Brent decided yogis and gurus were the greatest thing since sliced bread. At least it was not horrifically expensive to get into yoga, but Brent did manage to find an exclusive society for them to join where a high-flying swami bestowed words of wisdom on the upper crust. Since Sue felt she had to pay her own way in these ventures, she was kept sufficiently broke that she could hardly afford to travel from one end of San Francisco to the other, let alone all the way to Brynstol.

As for Jennifer's life in Squire House, after the

strange encounter that one afternoon, the house became exceptionally cold for about a week for no cause Jennifer or Innes could discover. She had the strange experience of needing to wear a heavy woolen sweater indoors in summer, and shedding it when she went outside.

Although the house eventually returned to normal, Jennifer's mind could not rest. She often dwelt on that afternoon, going over and over every word that had been spoken, trying to make rational sense out of it.

She had practically taken the house apart looking for a "secret passageway" of some sort— anything to explain how the stranger got into her house. It was useless; she couldn't find anything. How then did that man manage to spend enough time, unseen and unnoticed, near her in Squire House to find out so much about her? How did Jock and Beau come to know him so well? And, although she had never admitted it to herself, how was it that she knew there was something special about the big leather chair in the living room, as if it belonged to someone else, and that only he could use the chair? The smell of pipe tobacco, the occasional iciness in the air, she could go on and on, and for a while she did, until she decided the encounter had never happened. It was only a dream, so life-like that it seemed real, yet was the result of an over-active, romantic imagination. How could a ghost smoke a pipe anyway? The thought was ridiculous! Perhaps she was under some strange narcoleptic spell and lit it herself!

Or perhaps she was simply spending too much time alone.

She wished Sue could have spent time with her that summer in Brynstol. The mornings were cold and foggy, but by 11 a.m. the fog burned off and the sun shone as warmly and fully as anywhere. At about 5 p.m. the welcome fog came rolling in again to cool off people and animals from the heat of the day.

In time, Jennifer got over her uneasiness about the attic and often went up there to see what she could find. Beyond the paintings, there was little of interest. Jennifer took some of the linens that she, Ross and Sue had discovered earlier and washed them. They were far too lovely to be stashed away in an old trunk. Also, Jennifer found a place in the house for every one of Paul Squire's paintings except the one that resembled her. That picture made her uneasy, so it alone remained in the attic.

Yet, from time to time, she would go into the attic and study it. Paul Squire...no, the man *pretending to be* Paul Squire...had said he allowed her to stay in Squire House only because she reminded him of "her." So, who was she?

The woman had obviously been happy when the portrait was painted, and behind her were a beach and the ocean. It looked like the landscape near Squire House...and much like the beach in Jennifer's dream, the one in which she was frightened and running.

But that woman wasn't running. She was filled with joy.

Jennifer wondered if she, herself, had ever been that happy.

Her life had settled down considerably, but not completely. She still had the nagging feeling that something was wrong—something was just missing the mark, like a movie where the sound is ever so slightly out of sync with the video.

132 | Joanne Pence

Chapter 11

THE DOGS RAN to the front door. Gresham Innes had arrived for dinner, as he did at least once each week. Beau and Jock knew the sound of his car, and always greeted him as a long lost friend.

He called out hello to Jennifer as he entered the house—no one locked their doors in Brynstol.

"I'm in the living room, Mr. Innes," she replied.

He walked in waving a bottle of wine. "Charles Krug, sauvignon gris."

"How nice, but what's the occasion?" she asked.

"A beautiful meal and a beautiful woman. I said to myself a good bottle of wine would be the icing on the cake."

"Cake is what we're having for dessert."

Innes laughed and sat on the window seat looking out over the water. "Every time I come by I'm surprised all over again at what a marvelous job you have done here. You are very remarkable you know, my dear."

"Flattery will get you everywhere, but my chief accomplishment was to leave as much as possible as it was originally."

Nevertheless Jennifer was pleased by Innes' remarks and after a quick aperitif, she brought out dinner. The main course was a spinach soufflé made from her garden.

When the meal was over, content and satisfied, they retired to the living room with coffee and a pony glass of Benedictine, a prior gift from Innes to Jennifer.

Innes built a small fire in the fireplace, turned down the lights and put Elgar's Cello Concerto on the stereo. Their shared love of classical music was a joy to them both. The concerto evoked in Innes stories of the composer's life which he enjoyed relating to Jennifer. He often said he enjoyed talking to her about so many things, it was a marvel to him.

"Jennifer, I must tell you," he said, "these evenings here with you have been some of the happiest moments of my entire life."

"Thank you. It's very good of you to say that. I

enjoy them as well. You are the best company in all of Brynstol, if not the entire county!"

"My dear, come sit beside me." Innes motioned for Jennifer to join him on the sofa.

"All right." She moved to his side, somewhat baffled by the strange request.

Innes took her hand and held it in both of his. "I want to express to you, my dear, how very much you have come to mean to me over these past few months. Perhaps I should not speak. I'm an old man; I'm well aware of that. But maybe for that reason alone I need to say what is in my heart."

Jennifer felt decidedly awkward when Innes first took her hand, and by the end of his brief speech she wished he would say no more. The last thing she wanted was to hear a declaration of love, or any affection other than pure friendship. For him to pursue the matter would require her to declare a similar emotion or it would put such a strain on their relationship that further evenings together would be awkward, if not impossible.

"That's very kind," she said withdrawing her hand. "You are my dear friend, and our friendship is a true treasure to me, as I hope it is to you."

"Friendship—yes!" Innes face reddened, and he clasped his hands tightly together. "Friendship we have, my dear, for now, but the future! The fu—"

Innes' cup, which had sat on the coffee table before him, tipped over and coffee splashed all over his pants leg. *"Yeowww!"* He jumped up as rapidly as his aging body allowed.

"Oh dear!" Jennifer grabbed the napkins and gave them to him. "I hope you haven't been burned."

He held the soggy pants material away from his leg as he dabbed it with napkins. "Not…not too badly." He drew in his breath. "I'm afraid I've made a bit of a mess."

Jennifer got a wet cloth from the kitchen to wipe up the coffee from the carpet, but Innes took it and scrubbed the carpet himself. "I don't know what happened."

"Perhaps"—Jennifer wracked her brain—"I bumped the table by mistake."

"I didn't notice you move," Innes murmured. "I didn't notice anything move! Well, the carpet will survive, as will I. Let's put on some

Tchaikovsky."

As Innes took care of the CDs, Jennifer went to get more coffee for them. "I brought some more Benedictine, too," she said as she sat again. "After all that you might appreciate it."

"Oh, how good of you, my dear," Innes beamed. "How thoughtful! You are so good to me."

Jennifer sat in a chair away from him. They drank their coffee and liqueur in relative silence as Innes hoped that the peaceful, pleasant mood that had been created before his coffee spilled could develop again. The Benedictine gave him renewed confidence. This time, however, he decided he would move closer to Jennifer rather than vice versa, and scooted across the sofa to be near her. He looked at her tenderly, then took a deep breath. "My dear, words cannot express—"

He no sooner got those words out than he began to slide off the couch. *"Whoa, whoa, whooooaaa!"* he cried, hands flailing wildly to grab the back of the sofa when suddenly he landed on the floor.

"Who pushed me!" he yelled, looking up at her.

"Mr. Innes!" she cried, jumping to her feet.

He slowly stood, turning in a complete circle as if ready to combat whoever shoved him. No one was there but Jennifer. The look on his face went from anger, to confusion, to stark terror.

"I...I'm sorry," he mumbled. "I'm just not myself tonight." At that he turned and ran from the house.

Jennifer plopped herself back into the chair and sat in shock a moment before her lips widened in a smile that soon turned into a full-fledged laugh. She laughed until tears streamed down her eyes. "So you are still here, my invisible protector!" She stood and slowly pivoted in a circle as she spoke. "And you do still care despite all your harsh words! Well, thank you for helping me out of a potentially embarrassing situation. I'll visit Mr. Innes tomorrow, and I'm sure all will be forgotten. He'll chalk it up to too much wine. But I know why the coffee spilled, and why he fell off the sofa. Not very elegant, but it achieved the necessary result. So thank you."

Then Jennifer stopped, and wondered about herself. Maybe it was just the liquor that caused

Innes to spill his coffee and fall off the sofa. Here she was, making outlandish assumptions, along with talking to someone who didn't even exist. She must be quite insane, she decided. Absolutely, start raving mad!

She folded her arms. "If you are just a figment of my imagination, I am sorry. I think I should have liked to get to know you."

At that she shut the lights, called Beau and Jock into the house, locked the doors and jauntily went off to bed.

Chapter 12

THE NEXT MORNING, Jennifer went to Roundmore and Innes to see how Mr. Innes was feeling. He looked decidedly sheepish when he first saw her, but she acted as if a terrible accident had happened that caused him to fall through no fault of his own, and that she was exceedingly concerned about the state of his health. At this, Innes gallantly stated he was fine. They then were able to talk just like old times, and by the time Jennifer left she felt they were again good friends and nothing more.

She had stopped to see Innes while on her way to Mrs. Petris' place with Beau and Jock. Mrs. Petris had telephoned a few days earlier that she had decided to mate Beau to one of her loveliest females, and it was time to leave Beau with her to do his duty, so to speak.

When Jennifer and Jock left to return to Squire House, Jock was upset at leaving Beau behind, but obediently followed Jennifer.

When they reached Squire House, Jennifer

patted Jock. "I guess it's just you and me for a few days." At that, he went bounding off to check the grounds and to make sure nothing had been disturbed in his absence. It had normally been Beau's duty to peruse the grounds while Jock inspected the house whenever they had been away for any period of time.

Jennifer actually felt a little strange entering the house without Jock going first to be sure everything was as it should be.

She went straight down the hall to the kitchen and prepared an afternoon tea while she put away a couple of items she had bought in Brynstol. Then she picked up her cup of tea and the day's newspaper and headed towards the living room. As she approached it she stopped. The distinct scent of pipe tobacco was in the air. She felt her heart thrum with anticipation as she walked the rest of the way to the living room.

He was there. She stopped in the doorway, staring.

"If I'd known you were making tea I would have asked for a cup myself. It goes well with a pipe. I never really acquired a taste for coffee. It was considered a plebian brew, not nearly as popular as it is today. Although perhaps today there are simply more plebs?"

Jennifer felt light-headed but somehow managed to keep her composure. "The water is still hot; I'll make you a cup if you'd like."

"If it's no trouble."

She stared at him. "You won't go away?"

The man laughed, "But I never go away, you see!" He was still chuckling as Jennifer hurried off for his tea.

She stood in the kitchen breathing deeply, telling herself she was hallucinating even as she placed a tea bag in a cup and poured hot water over it. She carried the cup and saucer into the living room and placed them on the coffee table near the big leather chair.

Paul picked up the string and lifted the tea bag from the water. "Wasteful, but clever," he murmured.

"Take it out when the tea's the strength you want it," she said.

He gave her a wry glance. "So I assumed."

She nervously sat on the sofa, her eyes never

leaving him.

He removed the bag then lifted the cup to his lips.

"Be careful," she cried. "It's hot."

He cocked an eyebrow and took a sip. "Ah, a brew for the Gods. Forget nectar! How long it has been since I've tasted tea?"

"You don't drink tea...where you're from?" Jennifer asked cautiously.

"I don't need to drink anything," he replied. "I don't need to eat anything either, if you want to know."

Jennifer tried not to ponder that. She cleared her throat, then said, "May I ask something without you getting excited and carrying on like you did last time?"

One eyebrow lifted. "Me get excited and carry-on? How blatantly absurd. But I'll ignore your poor character analysis this time. Yes, you may ask anything you would like, and I will answer that which I choose. I believe that's a fair bargain, don't you?"

Instead of answering, or arguing, she said simply, "Why have you returned?"

"Why? The snippet asks why!" His voice dripped with disgust. "I was led to believe that my company was desired, that I was welcome here, and now I am so brazenly treated as to be asked why I've returned."

"You heard what I said last night." Jennifer was incredulous.

"Of course I heard. You were speaking to me, weren't you? Who else were you thanking? Just how many people do you think hang around this house anyway?"

"Then"—Jennifer was simultaneously smiling and yet so light-headed she could hardly get the words out—"you did do those things to Mr. Innes?"

"The old fool was making an ass out of himself. It was pitiful. The way he was going on he probably would have tried to molest you right here in my living room. If I were divested with a very sick sense of humor, I might have allowed the scene to continue. However, that is not my character. I determined it was best to stop it before it started."

Jennifer's blue eyes blazed in fury at the man.

"You have a very sick sense of humor! What gall! What nerve!"

"Is that any way to speak to the one who came to your rescue?" asked Paul seriously. "If you ask me, I'm a veritable knight in shining armor."

Jennifer stopped, stood up, her hand pressed to her forehead as she went to the window. "What am I doing? I'm here either talking to myself or to the world's best charlatan. There's no one else in this house. Right?"

"Wrong."

Jennifer spun around. "Who are you and what are you trying to do to me?"

"You know who I am, Jennifer. Sit down!" He leaned back in the chair and crossed one long leg over the other. "Such histrionics bore me to tears. Accept what your eyes and ears tell you is true. I, for one, am not trying to do anything but live in harmony and peace"—he steepled his hands together—"as befits my nature."

"You are not Paul Squire!"

"Wrong again."

"Paul Squire is dead!"

"Right, finally."

"You are not Paul Squire," she insisted.

"This is tedious. Hand me some paper Jennifer, and a fountain pen if you have one. Those new ball points allow no character to come through."

Jennifer found some paper and a gel pen. "It's not a fountain pen, but not a ball point either."

Paul picked it up and studied the strange tip, then tested it with a few scribbles. After a "harrumph," which Jennifer couldn't interpret, he signed his name with a flourish and then handed her the paper.

She walked to the bookshelf and took out one of Paul Squire's books. Opening the fly leaf she found a nameplate with his signature on it. The signatures looked the same.

"That book, by the way," Paul peering over her shoulder, "is full of underlining towards the end. An acquaintance once borrowed it and he had the nasty habit of underlining what he considered important. Either he considered nothing in the first two-thirds of the book of any importance or thought if he read only the end of it he didn't need to know what happened earlier. I never lent him another book."

Jennifer skittered away from him, strangely nonplussed by his nearness. Sure enough, as she flipped through the pages of the book there was no underlining in the first part, and quite a bit, in pencil, towards the back.

"And that one," he said pointing to a poetry collection, "has a light check-mark in pencil in the outer corner of page 23, where you'll find one of my favorite poems."

As he sat back in his leather chair, Jennifer opened the book and found the mark. "All right, I'll go along with you, for now," she said guardedly.

"Good, then let us put aside this nonsense. It is degrading and wasteful of our time. Time is a precious thing, which is a matter that you are too young as yet to realize."

She looked at the poem that was marked. It was by Emily Dickinson:

Of all the souls that stand create I have elected one

When sense from spirit flies away,
And subterfuge is done;

"I didn't realize men liked Dickinson. I think of her as a woman's poet," Jennifer commented.

"In my day—she and I were contemporaries—Dickinson was considered almost scandalous. How a woman could express such things about love, death, and the loneliness in life, was remarkable. Many people dismissed her poetry as the blitherings of a frustrated spinster."

"Spinsters are pathetic creatures, aren't we?" said Jennifer hotly. She returned the book to the shelf.

"Marriage is not for everyone, Jennifer. Some never have the luck to find the right person; some find that person and then lose him or her; and some simply are not interested in the marital institution. In any case, I'm just repeating what others said. Obviously I admire Dickinson. Some of her insights regarding death were wrong, but for one of this world she was remarkably sensitive about the other side."

"Hmm," Jennifer looked at him with suspicion again. She sat down once more on the sofa, but she simply could not get her mind to accept the preposterousness of all this. "You should tell me, now that you're here, how do you intend to live in this house? And...and how do I know where you are? I mean, when I can't see you…"

Paul roared with laughter at this. "My good woman, I am not a Peeping Tom. Have no fear. I respect your privacy."

She had to admit the situation was rather amusing, but at the same time, his laughing at her was more than a little annoying. "Do you need a bedroom? Or…or anything else? I mean, where do you sleep? And where do you go when I can't see you? I mean…this is all rather…" She knew she was babbling. Finally she gave up with a shake of the head.

"Please," he said, exasperated. "I've managed for decades without intruding on your life or anyone else's. I can do the same now. Although…" He turned thoughtful as he regarded her, then he stood and raked his hand through his hair. "God, I've been an idiot. How did I not consider your position in all this? A young woman, alone. It was wrong of me. I'm sorry, you see, I've come to feel I know you, being here with you. I never thought…I should go."

She stood as well. "I don't understand."

He cocked his head slightly, his pale gray eyes

sad and troubled. "Goodbye, Jennifer. You're free to live here as you please. I won't disturb you again."

He's leaving? After all this time trying to convince me he's real and should be welcome in this house, he's going to simply go away? He can't do that!

"Wait," she said, her word stopping him as he headed to the door.

"Yes?"

"You…you don't disturb me, Paul," she said. "You say you've gotten to know me over these past weeks, but don't you realize I've gotten to know you as well?"

Now it was his turn to look surprised.

"Of course I have." She stepped closer. "Living in your house, surrounded by your furniture, your books, your paintings. Each choice you've made tells me something about the man you are."

He said nothing for a moment, then, "They'd still be here, whether we meet or not."

She thought back on his choice of poetry, and capturing his eyes with hers softly confessed,

"Ghosts don't have the market cornered on loneliness, Paul."

"Don't we?" he whispered.

She took another step. "We'll work it out."

He rubbed his jaw. "I wouldn't mind trying," he admitted. "My life, death—hell, both—have been somewhat dull."

She smiled and, strangely, believed him. "Would you like some sherry?" she asked, thinking of another of Gresham Innes' gifts.

"That would be quite nice."

Jennifer went off to get glasses for the sherry, but when she returned the room was empty. Disappointment filled her.

She poured one glass and set it on the mantle. Why had he gone? Was it for good this time? Or was she simply going mad?

She faced the center of the room, and in a loud voice announced, "Perhaps this evening after dinner Mr. Squire will join me for some dessert and conversation."

Then, feeling decidedly foolish, she hurried outside to look for Jock.

Chapter 13

JENNIFER WAS NERVOUS after dinner. It was almost as if she were getting ready for a first date with a new beau. She glanced down at the grubby clothes that she had worn to bicycle up to the Petris kennels, to shop, and to work in the garden, and had a sudden desire to change into something feminine and pretty. How absolutely ridiculous! Here she was, a sensible, twenty-first century woman, over thirty years old, sitting around alone in her house thinking she should dress up for an apparition that was surely nothing but a creation of her overwrought imagination.

Since she was too young to be senile, her peculiar imaginings were surely an affliction caused by isolation. Hadn't she admitted her loneliness to the so-called "ghost"? She could see her epitaph now, "Here lies Jennifer Barrett, the mad hermit of Brynstol."

On the other hand, this was her daydream and if she wanted to dress up for it, why not? Who was to stop her?

She showered and washed her hair, then chose one of her most alluring dresses, a yellow floral print, sleeveless, with a plunging V-neckline that would show off her newly acquired tan. She dried and flat-ironed her hair until it fell shiny and sleek over her shoulders.

In the living room, she put a recording of Rachmaninoff's second piano concerto—the one whose big melody was lifted for the pop song "Full Moon and Empty Arms." That was surely appropriate, she thought, not missing the irony of the title.

With the book of poetry she had looked at earlier in hand, she sat in one of the large chairs and began to read.

When an hour went by she wondered if she wasn't going to be stood up by her own imagination. After another hour, as Rimsky-Korsakov's *Scheherazade* played, she decided she must be the most foolish creature on the face of the earth. At least she was able to take some comfort in enjoying the poetry. She thought she probably ought to just go upstairs to bed and forget all this foolishness, but she decided to read a bit more before that. The time passed slowly and she felt sleepier and sleepier…

She heard a light cough and opened her eyes to see Paul Squire standing by the fireplace.

"Good evening," was all Jennifer said, trying to hide her surprise as her drowsiness vanished.

"You look very lovely tonight," Paul said with a rare smile. He had a very nice smile, she noticed, one that caused his gray eyes to twinkle. Who ever thought a ghost could have sparkling eyes? She was obviously mad as a hatter, and yet, when she looked at him, her heart did a two-step.

"*Scheherazade?*" he said. "Are you planning to captivate me with a tall tale each evening?"

"Or is it vice versa?" she said.

He chuckled as he sat in the chair opposite her. "Do you mind if I smoke?" he asked, taking his pipe and tobacco pouch out of his jacket pocket.

"It's your home," she admitted.

He filled his pipe, leaned back and soon the smoke circled him.

Jennifer didn't quite know how to phrase her curiosity at his obvious enjoyment of the pipe, but finally she said, "I would have thought such worldly things would not be of any interest to you anymore."

"What could be more ethereal than smoke?" Paul replied. "Besides, I like the taste. In my day, it was something a man could enjoy and feel no shame in, as I've heard is the situation today."

"True," she said with a nod.

He puffed a few more times, then said, "I've always felt this house should have more than one person in it."

"It would have been a fine home for a family," Jennifer agreed. "How did you come to build it?"

"It's a fairly lengthy story." Paul waved his pipe dismissively. "Suffice it for the moment to say that when I built it, it was not my intention to live alone. But life is full of the unexpected, as I learned much to my unhappiness and eventually to my ruin."

"But I am interested in your story," she said. "Very interested, if you would like to tell it to me. I…I can't help but imagine it has something to do with the portrait of the woman who resembles me."

He looked momentarily startled, but then

nodded with resignation. "Ah, yes. I'm not surprised to hear you say that."

"I've made some assumptions about her. I wonder if I'm right."

"You make it sound like a scientific experiment," he said with an amused smirk.

She laughed. "Believe me, there is nothing scientific about this conversation! But seriously, I am interested in you. And her. I wish you would tell me about you both."

He took a few more puffs. "They always say the best way to flatter the male ego is for a woman to beg him to talk about himself. But not now. I'd much rather hear about you."

She spent that evening telling him about her life, which she considered dull, and he seemed to find fascinating.

The next night, after dinner, he visited her again, this time filled with curiosity about her CD player. "I enjoy symphonies and concertos," he said. "But I had to go to a concert hall to hear them. To have so much music come from a small silver disk is beyond my comprehension. Do you play any instrument?"

"Me? Oh…once, but no more," she replied.

"Why not? What was it?" he asked.

"A violin. I wasn't any good, however. When I'd practice, my mother would run around the house with her fingers in her ears and ask who was killing cats!" She smiled wryly. "It took a few years, but eventually I got the message."

"I'm sorry to hear that," he said. "The violin has always been one of my favorite instruments. I don't suppose you sing?"

She chuckled. "Not a note."

"I guess I'll never hear opera again," he said rather morosely.

"Why not?" she pointed at her opera collection.

"Those? Really? You mean you I would be able to hear an entire opera here, now?" He was stunned.

"Which is your favorite? I might have it."

He pondered this a moment. "I can think of one that seems particularly appropriate given my current state. I wonder if you know it—Richard Wagner, *The Flying Dutchman*. It's about a ghost captain doomed to roam the earth forever in his phantom ship. Clearly," he added with a smile, "a man after my own heart."

She knew the opera. What he didn't say was that the story's theme was redemption through love, that only by finding the love of a good and true woman could the ghostly captain's curse be removed. "Ask and you shall receive." She found the opera and put it on her stereo, much to Paul Squire's delight and astonishment.

After that, he returned night after night. He had opinions on everything, and there was much he wanted to learn about.

Picasso, Dali, Klee, Miro were a whole new art world to him. He was like a man who was ravenous, and stumbled upon a banquet. Jennifer resorted to the mobile lending library to get books to try to answer many of the questions he had.

No sooner did he learn something new than he would form an opinion on it and passionately argued in favor of however he decided things "should" be. A most exasperatingly arrogant man, she thought, although she also found him completely intriguing. They would talk late into the night when she would begin to fade with fatigue, and oddly, he would seem to physically fade a bit. He always bid her good night soon after that. She decided her eyes must play tricks on her when the hour grew late.

Yet, despite their many talks and her many questions, he never spoke of his days on earth, and never told her about the woman in the portrait.

Chapter 14

FOR THE FIRST TIME in her life Jennifer was not sure she was happy with the prospect of her friend Sue visiting. Sue planned to spend the Thanksgiving holidays with her, arriving late Wednesday and staying until the following Tuesday. To Jennifer that meant six days of not seeing Paul Squire. She knew there was no way she could spring Paul on Sue, even if he were to agree. Nor would she want to. Sue would cart her off to a looney bin.

Jennifer wondered if perhaps her experience was not as unique as she had thought, but if strictly for the reasons she had just considered no one would admit to any sort of communication with the other side. She would have to ask Paul that question, and hopefully he would answer, although he still steadfastly refused to discuss why he had returned to Squire House after death, and why he was there to this day.

In truth, whatever the reason, all that mattered

to her was that he was there, and they were together. It was a startlingly new feeling for her, this sense of togetherness. She had spent a lifetime feeling like the 'odd man out,' the loner who could never find a person to be completely comfortable with, who never found a person to love.

Now, there was…what? A ghost? A figment of her imagination? The product of too many books read and movies watched by a lonely, unloved and unlovable woman?

She couldn't believe he was only that, and yet her practical side told her he couldn't be anything else, and definitely couldn't be what he claimed.

Practical, be hanged. Whatever he was, she cared about him. With him, her days were filled with laughter and wit and companionship. And perhaps, a little at least, with love.

Jennifer stopped at Roundmore and Innes to invite Innes to Thanksgiving dinner with her and Sue. Although pleased with the invitation, Innes was clearly hurt by the way Jennifer had ignored him lately. He had only been to Squire House once for dinner in the past four weeks. His last visit, unbeknownst to Innes, had caused Jennifer a tiff with Paul. He didn't want Innes to return to "his" house, but Jennifer had insisted because Innes was her friend. Jennifer got her way and invited Innes to dinner, but Paul then proceeded to mischievously harass her throughout the evening with escapades behind Innes' back. Dishes twirled mysteriously in the air as Innes sat obliviously talking. A linen napkin floated about the room, even proceeding to do somersaults. Jennifer nearly died between suppressing laughter and fearing that Innes would notice the shenanigans. As a result, she paid very little attention to him or to his conversation. He remarked several times that she seemed distant, as if her mind were elsewhere. She tried to assure him it was not and that she was quite interested in all that was taking place that evening—and she did mean *all*. Finally, Innes left. Then, to top it off, Paul showed his indignation by not visiting her the next two evenings.

She had planned on being angry with him over such childish behavior, but when he didn't appear the second night, she feared she had truly offended him. When he finally showed himself the third night she was so relieved she found herself apologizing to him! How he enjoyed that! He relished every word she spoke and then imperiously forgave her for her loyalty to her old friend, misplaced though he considered it to be. Then, while Jennifer held her tongue for fear of starting another row, Paul went so far as to say that someday she might even invite Innes over again.

She laughed inwardly at how very different nineteenth century men were from those of the twenty-first century, but despite his imperious pronouncements, she knew he regarded her well. In fact, she believed he held her in higher regard than anyone she had ever known. In what was also very nineteenth century, he practically put her on a pedestal. She felt awkward about it, but at the same time, discovered that a chivalrous man wasn't necessarily a bad thing.

But now she faced a new dilemma with no idea of Paul's reaction to Sue's visit. He once said something about liking her—but for six days? Jennifer dreaded telling him.

In for a dime, in for a dollar, she decided, which led to her inviting Innes and also Ross Alderworth to the Thanksgiving dinner. When she phoned Clevewick and asked to speak to Ross, she was surprised at how quickly the person who answered the residential telephone located him. She told him Sue would be visiting from San Francisco. He hesitated, as if he had plans for the day, but then said he would love to join them at dinner.

Finally, the day arrived when she could no longer delay telling Paul about the many people who would be visiting Squire House. By the time the hour of Paul Squire's visit arrived, she was a bundle of nerves.

She sat in a chair attempting to read a book when Paul entered the room.

"You look as nervous as a cat!" he said immediately.

"A fine way to greet me!"

He sat in his favorite chair and lit his pipe. "What's on your mind, Jennifer?"

She poured him a scotch on the rocks—a recently acquired taste.

His brows rose and she handed it to him. "I guess this means trouble," he muttered.

"No, no trouble. I heard from my old friend Sue today."

"And how is old Sue?" Paul interrupted jokingly.

"Sue is fine! So fine, in fact, she's taken some time off to come visit."

"To visit? You mean to stay here for a day or two?" Paul asked.

"A little bit longer," she said hurriedly. "But it'll be so nice for me to see Sue again! The last time she was here was the spring. She's a great girl, lots of fun. You liked her, didn't you?"

"I dare say I am getting the impression that it doesn't matter what I like or what I say about this. But, since you've asked, I definitely do not like her."

"You don't?" Jennifer could hardly believe anyone not liking Sue. "Why not?"

"Because of her intrusion into my household. Doesn't she have anything better to do than to drive up here at the drop of a hat?"

"Be reasonable," Jennifer cried. "You know that isn't true. She's only been here once ages ago. My God, how you do go on!"

"I go on? Me?" He jumped to his feet and paced in front of the fireplace. "Now I am to put up with even more intruders in my midst. More than two days you said? How abominable! How I detest these intrusions! It was bad enough to allow one giddy female into my life here, now she's bringing her friends. Soon they'll infest the place like so many cockroaches!

"Then, what next?" He dropped into the leather chair in a huff, head back, his hands pressed to his forehead, elbows out. "As your friends get older they'll start to breed and multiply! They'll bring their sniveling, dirty little brats with them here where they'll run around with their sticky fingers touching into all my things. A trail of mud will mark where the snotty, slimy little..."

"All right, all right!" interrupted Jennifer. "Must you make a federal case out of everything? It's only for six days, starting Wednesday night. It's just Sue, and she is still single!"

"Six days? *Six days!*" He jumped to his feet, walking in circles, arms waving. "Do you realize how long six days is in the life of a man? A very large percentage! In the life of a fly it's, it's probably two lifetimes!" He went on muttering to himself about ants, worms, caterpillars.

"Wednesday, you said?" he turned to Jennifer again. "She doesn't give bloody much warning does she? Some friends you have! Come moving in, uninvited. Why don't you choose your friends better?"

Jennifer was also on her feet now, fists to hips. "Choose my friends! What friends? The only real friends I have are Sue and Mr. Innes, and you act like a raving maniac whenever I want to see either one of them! Who do you think you are?"

"If you think I care a fig about whom you see and do not see, you are sadly mistaken!" Paul stood still and clamped his pipe between his teeth.

"Well, good." Jennifer took a step closer to him. Softly and sweetly she smiled up at him and in a voice dripping with honey said "I'm glad you feel that way because then you'll not care that I've invited both my friends and Ross Alderworth here for Thanksgiving dinner."

He slowly removed the pipe, his voice a low, slow growl. "You didn't!"

"I did."

"How low!"

She folded her arms, head cocked in what she

realized was a Paul-like stance. "I don't consider it such. I think it shall be a lovely dinner."

"And if I don't agree?" Paul threatened.

She waggled her finger in front of his face. "Paul Squire, if you do anything, anything whatsoever to ruin this dinner so help me I'll never speak to you again! I'll hate you until the day I die! I'll think of something to do to you!"

He gave a theatrical sigh. "I see. You have chosen your philistine friends over me. Then my presence is no longer needed, and obviously not welcome here." At that he started towards the door.

"Paul," said Jennifer.

He stopped and turned. "Yes?"

She smiled. "Sue will be gone next Wednesday."

An eyebrow lifted. "Humph!" He snorted, turned, and walked out of the room.

"Damn," thought Jennifer. She had been hoping to spend this evening and the next evening with Paul before Sue arrived the following day. She knew she had to tell him tonight about the visit, though, or he would have found out anyway. He always does.

It was strange, she thought, she had always been rather tongue-tied and awkward in a man's presence, yet with Paul she was not only able to converse, but also to speak her mind when necessary. If they argued that was okay too because she felt that deep down the bond between them had grown so great, and the understanding so complete, that no mere argument could break it. She felt sure of herself with a man for the first time in her life and sure enough of Paul's feeling for her that she knew he would be back. She didn't know when—he was an obstinate creature—but he would be back.

Chapter 15

DESPITE THE ARGUMENT with Paul, Jennifer was able to go about the next two days preparing for Sue's visit with a basically light heart. She missed him, but finally Wednesday, and company, arrived.

Mr. Innes showed up in the morning with a turkey. He had insisted on providing it. It was a lovely turkey, twenty pounds, a goodly amount for four people, but then Jennifer did have a store of leftover turkey recipes to fall back on. She couldn't help but wonder if this wasn't Innes' way of inviting himself back for another meal, especially when he started talking about how much he liked turkey soup.

Innes drove Jennifer back to town with him where she was able to pick up a few last minute items, and then he most willingly returned with her to Squire House. He seemed willing to stay with her as she waited for Sue, but Jennifer quickly thanked him for the ride and said goodbye before he got a chance to invite himself inside.

The wait was much longer than Jennifer had expected, and evening came before Beau and Jock scrambled, barking, to the front door. Jennifer went to the window and sure enough, there was the little blue sports car that had brought Sue to Brynstol months earlier.

Sue stepped out of the passenger side of the car and a tall, good-looking man got out of the driver's side. From Sue's descriptions of Brent Cooper with his sandy hair and light blue eyes, Jennifer needed no introduction. She was briefly taken aback, but her pleasure at seeing her friend overcame all other emotions and she hurried from the house to give Sue a big hug.

The two women laughed and giggled like schoolgirls over being together again, and then Sue introduced Jennifer to Brent.

"Welcome to Squire House," Jennifer said, "What a nice surprise."

"I hope I won't inconvenience you. It wasn't until the last minute that Sue decided I should come along."

"No inconvenience at all," Jennifer said. "I'm

glad to finally meet you!"

Sue explained further. "Brent was set up to go with an encounter group to Monterey for the weekend, but then the group fell through, so he would have been left alone for the holiday."

"Not the group, Sue," said Brent sounding slightly perturbed. "The meeting was all that didn't pan out."

"Well, whatever." Sue turned back to Jennifer. "Here we are!"

The women laughed again, and all joined in picking up luggage and other packages and carried them into the house.

Jennifer showed Brent and Sue to their room, and went downstairs to make some coffee as the two freshened up from their trip. Brent's arrival was an unexpected turn of events. She had hoped to be able to spend hours talking to Sue the way they used to do, but guessed that wouldn't happen during this visit. She was interested, however, in getting to know Brent. Reading between the lines of Sue's letters, her impression of him was negative. She hoped that in person he would assuage her anxiety. Jennifer loved Sue like a sister, and she wanted only what was best for Sue in everything.

Sue and Brent soon came downstairs and joined Jennifer in the living room. Brent didn't sit, as Sue did, but instead walked around taking in every detail. Finally, he spoke, "This is truly a lovely home, Jennifer. I didn't expect to find such quality of workmanship."

"Thank you. I find it extraordinary as well. It was designed and built with much care. There aren't many places like it around here."

"But there are a few," Sue said. "Last time I was here Jennifer and I rode around and found some really nice places. Clevewick was one. It was beautiful."

"What's Clevewick?" asked Brent.

"It's a large ranch, mainly for dairy products," explained Jennifer. "That reminds me! Guess who's coming to Thanksgiving dinner with us tomorrow?"

"Ross?" Sue asked.

"That's right! And Gresham Innes is also invited."

Sue was pleased at this news. "How nice it will

be to see them both."

Brent looked at the two and raised his eyebrows. "Two men invited for two women? It seems I am interrupting something."

"Oh, no!" Jennifer laughed.

"Silly!" said Sue. "Mr. Innes is old as the hills and Ross is just a friend of ours."

"Also old?" Brent asked,

"No, he's young. He works at Clevewick."

"Ah, the connection!" said Brent.

"Anyway, I'm sure you'll like both of them," Sue said.

Brent stood up, "Well, if I'm going to be in any shape to meet anybody tomorrow I had better get some sleep. That drive up here is a killer!"

"I'll be up shortly," Sue said. "I'd like to talk to Jennifer a while."

"Sure, no hurry. Jennifer, good night. Thank you for your hospitality."

"You're very welcome," Jennifer replied. "Good night, Brent."

Brent went up the stairs and when he was heard shutting the bedroom door Sue spun toward Jennifer. "I hope you don't mind my asking Brent to join us. I really didn't know what to do. I hated the thought of leaving him alone for four days or more. I just would worry too much and not know what to expect when I got back."

"I'm not sure what you mean by all that, but Brent is most welcome. He seems like a nice fellow."

Sue's brow furrowed. "He is. I'm afraid I expect too much sometimes. It's not Brent's fault. It's my fault. I'm sure of that."

"Do you want to tell me what the problem is?" asked Jennifer.

"It's so dumb, I hate to say anything. I sound like an idiot complaining about Brent. I mean he's a marvelous guy. He's got good looks, brains, money. What more could a person ask for?"

"That sounds pretty overwhelming." Jennifer agreed. "But something is troubling you. And if it is, it's better to talk about it than to keep it inside. Sometimes, if you talk you'll see that you can either work it out, learn to accept it, or get out of the situation."

Sue stood up. "It's really nothing. I'm being silly. That's all. Let's forget it. Maybe I had better get upstairs."

Jennifer was silent for a moment then said, "In your letters you've mentioned Brent's habit of finding new interests, one after the other, in rapid succession without ever really getting deeply into anything. That seems to bother you."

Sue sat back down. "I shouldn't let it, should I? I mean, lots of people are that way at first. Brent enjoys finding new enthusiasms. It's better than being dull, right? So we keep trying new things. At times…well, anyway, Brent's idea is that happiness comes from doing something you enjoy, that life is all about trying new things, new adventures. Maybe he's right? The theory sounds plausible, doesn't it?"

"I'm not so sure," Jennifer admitted. "He seems to try lots of new things. When he does, is he happy?"

"That's the problem," Sue said. "He's not. Since he expects so much out of each new enthusiasm, when it doesn't live up to expectations, he's disappointed. Like the time he took up weightlifting…how many people have found true happiness in a barbell? Well, neither did Brent. But instead of seeing some value in trying to lift the barbell—building good health, strengthening muscles, what have you—when it didn't make him 'happy' he abandoned it completely! And he's that way with everything."

"But he must be satisfied with you?" Jennifer asked.

Sue took a deep breath before replying. "Sometimes I wonder. At least I'm not stuffed in the spare bedroom with the weight lifting equipment, the scuba gear, the guitar, the squash rackets, the jogging shoes, the rock collection, the stamp collection, and on and on."

"My God!" Jennifer laughed.

"It is rather funny, isn't it? I can see it now: someday he may become 'into' marriage. We get married, have a kid; then, one day I'll come home and say, 'Where's Junior?' And Brent will reply, 'Oh I got tired of him and stuck him in the spare bedroom.' What can you do?" Sue shrugged.

"Sue, you're too much!"

"Yeah, leave it to me to fall for the loonies. He sure is cute though, and sexy!"

"He might come around some day."

"That's what I keep hoping. Hell, he'll run out of new crazes eventually! But enough about me. What have you been up to all these months, Jenny?"

Jennifer told Sue a little bit about her life in Brynstol, omitting Paul Squire of course. Beau had become a father a short while back, and Jennifer had been spending time helping Mrs. Petris with the puppies. It was quite a chore keeping the kennel in order, and when a dog was going to be placed in a show it involved a couple of weeks work getting the coat to look just right. Mrs. Petris already owned a number of champion dogs and she was working on getting championships for more of them. She would get the dogs ready for the show, then send them off with a professional handler who would present each dog in the show ring. Mrs. Petris was so pleased by Jock's looks that she wanted to try showing him to see if he could become a champion as well. Since Brynstol was so out of the way, once a handler took one of Mrs. Petris' dogs they'd often keep it for a month or more, riding to a number of circuits throughout the Western states during that period. Jennifer hated the idea of such a long separation.

Mrs. Petris suggested Jennifer go along as well. She could even take Beau. That way she could see new towns and meet new people instead of staying in a lonely old house all by herself.

"I can't help but agree," Sue said. "I'm a little worried about your solitude. A little is fine, but you seem to have few friends. You need someone to talk to Jenny."

Jennifer shrugged. "When I want friends, I'll find them. Right now, I'm happy."

Sue didn't look convinced. "I'm sorry nothing worked out with Ross Alderworth."

"Don't worry about me," Jennifer said. "I see people in town. It's a small group, but I like them. They're enough to keep me happy for now. When they're not, I'll get a car. Or I'll get on Facebook. I know some people on it have thousands of friends."

"Very funny!" Sue said with a frown.

Chapter 16

ON THANKSGIVING MORNING the sun was shining brightly as it so often will do in the perverse northern California climate, where summer mornings are almost always overcast and foggy, while early winter days are clear and bright, and the best time of the year is autumn.

Jennifer rose early and went to the window overlooking the ocean. The view was the same as always. In this land of evergreens there were no true seasons. Rarely did it get very hot or very cold. Jennifer didn't mind since she grew up in San Francisco where the differences throughout the year were even less pronounced than in Brynstol. Jennifer had been here over eight months now. Come spring it would be a year. Her little garden had finally ceased to produce any food. She had canned and dried a good portion of its output and expected a good winter for herself.

She dressed quickly and went downstairs and put on coffee. It had just finished brewing when

Brent walked into the kitchen.

"Good morning," he said brightly.

"Hi. You sound chipper."

"I slept really well. It's so quiet up here, who wouldn't?"

"Would you like some coffee?"

"Great."

"Toast?"

"That would be fine. Looks like homemade bread?"

"Yes, one of many economies."

"'Economy, nothing—it's the best bread in the world!"

Jennifer laughed as she made them both bacon and eggs. Brent was clearly hungry as he polished off the meal in a matter of seconds.

"Do you ever miss the big city, Jennifer?" he asked, settling back with his coffee.

"Sometimes I do. I used to go to the movies, theater. I love the symphony, and occasionally I'd see an opera—although they're god-awful expensive. At times I'd go shopping and wander around stores and look at all the things I'd like to buy if only I were rich enough."

"Life is pretty different up here."

"Yes," Jennifer mused, "but less frustrating. Since I don't see anything to buy, I don't feel badly that I can't afford it!"

Brent caught her gaze and smiled. Jennifer stepped back from the power of it. As Sue had told her more than once, his smile was dazzling. "I see," he murmured.

"But I do miss seeing the city. I'll have to take a trip down soon."

"Yes, you should do so," Brent said with a surprising amount of enthusiasm. "But you have adapted very well to this way of life."

"I'm content."

"Content…" The word hung in the air, as if it was some new, startling revelation to him. "That's a very lucky thing to feel, Jennifer. I'm afraid it something I've never been able to find." He stood and walked to the window, looking out at the coast. When he spoke, it was more to himself than in conversation. "I wonder if anyone can so adapt."

Jennifer stepped to his side. "I rather doubt it. It's quiet; too quiet for most people. For someone like you, I suspect you'd die of boredom in a week's time. I know from Sue that you like to get involved in many things."

"I do, but…I don't know. No matter what I try I find no real pleasure." He met her gaze and she felt the full power of his all-too-perfect good looks, of his intense, soulful eyes. "None of it has meaning."

She swallowed hard, feeling awkward and a little stunned by the way he looked at her. "I'm sorry, Brent. Sorry for you."

He turned again to look out at the coast, and Jennifer felt as if she could breathe once more. "Maybe someplace like this, out of the world as I know it, everything would seem different. Better."

"I don't know if Sue is ready for this, either." Jennifer frowned, worried. "She sees herself as cosmopolitan, and likes the kind of world that one finds in the city, as do you, I believe. I think a person has to find what he needs within himself. No person, place, or thing can give it to you."

Brent faced Jennifer once more, leaned back against the counter, one ankle crossed over the other. He seemed to study her a moment, then said, "You're right."

"What's right?" Sue said as she stepped into the room, then yawned. "Oh, my, excuse me! What early birds you both are! This kitchen smells delicious! Umm, coffee—that's what I need."

Jennifer hurried across the kitchen to a cabinet and got a mug for her friend.

Sue looked from Jennifer to Brent. "You two were surely engrossed talking about something!"

"Just trying to solve the world's problems," Jennifer said. "I have a hundred and one things to do, so if you'll both excuse me, I had better get started."

She concentrated on making the turkey stuffing and before long both Sue and Brent joined in and did their share. Brent was fascinated by each step in the dinner preparation, including baking a pie filled with peaches Jennifer had canned earlier in the year. Jennifer suspected he had never had a meal like the one she was preparing, and he verified that after his grandparents died when he was young, he and his divorced mother ate Thanksgiving dinners in restaurants.

Before they knew it, it was time to get dressed for the holiday dinner.

Sue and Brent went off to get ready first, while Jennifer took care of last minute preparations. As a result, she was still upstairs dressing when Mr. Innes arrived.

He was quite pleased to meet Brent, and to see Sue again. He had settled in the living room when someone knocked at the front door.

Sue hurried to the door. There, just as she remembered him, stood Ross Alderworth. "Ross, how good to see you!"

"You look lovelier than ever, Sue," he said, handing her one of the two bundles of roses he carried.

"You are as charming as ever," Sue said, pleased at the thoughtful gift. She held out her hand for a friendly clasp, but Ross kept holding it as she led him into the house.

"Jennifer is still getting ready. She'll be downstairs in a minute," Sue explained. As they stepped into the living room, Brent rose. Sue pulled her hand free.

Ross nodded in greeting to Mr. Innes, then turned his attention to Brent, as Sue introduced the two.

Brent spoke first, "Pleased to meet you."

"Same here." Ross shook his hand, then somewhat hesitatingly asked, "Are you an old friend of Jennifer's?"

"No," Brent replied. "I just met her yesterday. I came up from the city with Sue."

"Oh, I see," said Ross rather quietly. He made a quick glance in Sue's direction, then strode across the room and sat down. Sue looked at him in some surprise, while Brent looked smug.

A silence settled on the room, while Sue rushed off to the kitchen to find vases.

"Well, well, well," said Innes at a loss for words. "How nice that we can all spend this holiday together!"

"Is it?" Ross asked.

"Absolutely!" Innes then launched into a long discourse on the state of realty within a hundred miles of Brynstol as Sue stepped into the room and sat by Brent. She interjected appropriate comments to keep Innes talking.

All at once Sue noticed a surprised look on Brent's face and then he smiled and stood up, all the while looking in the direction of the doorway.

Sue turned around to see what pleased him so and discovered that it was Jennifer. Or seemed to be Jennifer, although she herself had never seen her friend look that way before. The biggest change was in her hairstyle. Jennifer had usually worn her hair pulled straight back in a ponytail or twist, but today she wore the twist much higher and made it into a stylish swirl. Short wisps of hair had been curled to frame her face and fall lightly on the back of her neck in a delicate and feminine fashion.

Her dress was cream color with an elaborate bodice of muslin and lace giving it an almost Victorian look.

"Ross, Mr. Innes, I'm so glad you're here," she said. Her eyes caught those of Innes and Ross. She noticed that Ross was looking at her quite strangely.

"I was glad to be invited!" laughed Innes. "And I must say, you look beautiful tonight! Absolutely beautiful!"

"Thank you," she said, her cheeks slightly reddened.

"It's been a long time, Jen," said Ross.

"Too long, I think," added Jennifer, feeling

somewhat uncomfortable by his stare. "Roses! You brought them, didn't you, Ross? They're beautiful! Thank you."

He smiled and nodded.

"Jenny, I love your hair that way!" Sue said. "And that dress! It's great. Where did you ever find it?"

"It was in a shop in the town just north of Brynstol. A couple of the local ladies invited me to go with them. It must have been hanging there for fifty years, judging by the price. But I liked it."

"Jennifer," said Brent as he crossed the room to take her arm and guide her to a chair, "may I offer you something to drink?"

"Yes, thank you," she said.

Brent made her a martini. He and Sue brought a good supply of liquor with them from San Francisco, along with olives and onions.

As she sipped it she caught Ross' eye again. "You look at me so strangely Ross," Jennifer said.

"It's just that you remind me of someone, it seems. I can't remember who..."

"You know you're right!" said Sue. "There is something about the way Jennifer looks tonight.

What can it be?"

"You're both being silly," exclaimed Jennifer. "No more of this nonsense about me or I'll go change. I never dreamed getting dressed up would cause such a stir! Am I always so scruffy? My goodness!"

"You remind me of no one but your lovely self," said Innes, and they all laughed.

"It's the picture!" Ross exclaimed. All eyes turned to him. "You remember, Sue, don't you?"

Sue looked startled, than agreed. "Yes. You're right. How extraordinary." She looked at Jennifer in a most puzzled way.

"This is foolishness. Stop already!" Jennifer was getting noticeably upset by all this.

"What picture?" Brent asked Sue.

"Yes, yes," added Innes, "what picture? How juicily mysterious!"

"It's a Paul Squire portrait," explained Sue. "It's up in the attic. It looks just like Jennifer, especially today."

"Paul Squire—as in Squire House?" asked Brent. "You mean the first owner of this house was an artist?"

"That's right," Jennifer said. "The paintings that you see throughout the house are all his."

"Including the portrait in the attic," said Sue with a knowing nod.

"Let's have a look at it," Innes said, rubbing his hands together.

"No!" Jennifer stood up. "Don't be silly. I've looked at that painting time and again. There's minimal resemblance—minimal! After all, I'm a distant relative of Paul Squire's and I suspect the woman in the portrait is as well. Uh, *was* as well. Anyway, it's a very poor painting which is why I'm not displaying it. It does not do justice to the artist."

Just then, the painting of the fishermen fell off the wall with a crash. Everyone jumped.

Brent walked over and picked up the painting. "There's no harm done. And…how strange! The nail is still in the wall." He rehung it.

"Oh!" Jennifer cried. "My fault. I knew I hadn't hung it quite right."

Ross and Sue looked at each other.

Innes looked nervous. He gave a small cough. "Well, back to the portrait in the attic. I'm sure it's a fine painting. And all the better if it resembles

Jennifer, even in a small way."

Jennifer glared at him, but then forced a laugh. "Don't listen to them. They're being silly."

Sue picked up on Jennifer's attempt to change her mood. "If you think we're being silly, you should have heard everyone at work when I got my hair cut. They all said I reminded them of a poodle. A poodle in need of a trim, in fact, which added insult to injury. They carried on so much I was nearly in tears. Then, after I was thoroughly upset, they said they were kidding and they liked my hairdo. Some joke!"

"I hope Jennifer never cuts a hair on her head," Brent said, looking starry-eyed at his hostess.

Ross studied Sue to see how she was taking this, but she seemed unconcerned.

Jennifer stood up, "You people are all quite mad! I'm going to go put dinner on the table."

"I'll help!" Sue said.

The dinner was delicious and met with everyone's enjoyment. Although Brent and Ross eyed each other with hostility, Brent was interested in life in Brynstol, and particularly in Ross' stories about dairy farming. Innes relished playing the grand old man of the party, and by the time the evening was drawing to a close he had set himself up as a sort of patriarch over the small group. He decided that due to Brent's extreme interest in farming, and because Jennifer and Sue had never seen Clevewick, that Ross should give the three of them a tour the next day. Ross was amenable, and said he would come by the next morning to pick them up.

They chatted awhile longer. Brent and Sue talked about the latest fads in the city, and what was currently popular on stage and in the night spots. It sounded like a different world to Innes, who had gone to San Francisco only on brief visits. Ross, it turned out, had actually lived there for four years while he was a student at the University of San Francisco majoring in business administration. Sue and Jennifer realized they had been wrong about Ross being a hired hand at Clevewick—not with his education or with the price of the private university.

Finally, Ross and Innes decided that it was time for them to leave. With reminders that they would meet the next day (except for Innes, who had to work), they said good night.

Jennifer and Sue picked up a bit of the mess from the party, but both agreed they were too tired to do much in the way of cleaning up that evening. Sue and Brent soon retired. Jennifer said she, too, would be upstairs shortly.

After she heard the two settle down for the night, she prepared two cups of tea and carried them into the living room. She poured a glass of sherry and set it beside one teacup on the little table next to the large leather chair.

"Happy Thanksgiving to you, Paul," she said, as she took a sip of her tea. Then she set down her cup and stood, looking around the large, empty room. She walked to the seascape hanging over the mantelpiece. She looked up at the painting, and touched it lightly with her fingertips.

"Don't be angry with me any longer, Paul," she said to the painting, not knowing where else to address her words. "I missed you today. If you could have been with us, my day would have been complete. The combination of all those people, dear friends though they are, wasn't as much pleasure to me as spending time with you."

She chuckled to herself with a shake of her head. "I guess, all in all, I should hope you aren't nearby and haven't heard me. Your ego is already big enough!" Her voice softened. "But I do wish you were here, nonetheless."

At that Jennifer folded her arms on the mantelpiece and laid her forehead onto them. She was more than a little upset by her feelings. She had hoped that being around real people would make her forget all about Paul Squire, whoever or whatever he was. But instead she realized his worth more than ever. She felt, almost, as if she were falling in love with him. But that was impossible, crazy.

"How kind of you to bring me tea and sherry."

The voice she knew better than her own pierced her heart. She turned around, and saw him in his chair, the stemmed sherry glass in his hand.

"Paul!" she cried and rushed to his side. She knelt down on the floor beside the arm of his chair.

"My goodness," he said, "what's all this?"

"I've missed you."

"You flatter me. But you seemed quite a hit with everyone."

"I wish you could have joined us."

Paul laughed silently. "That would have made for a most memorable holiday!"

"I know it's impossible. That's the trouble." Her emotions raw, Jennifer stood up and turned her back to him, not wanting him to see her this way.

"You look very beautiful today, Jennifer. More than ever."

She squared her shoulder, head high. "Like…like the woman in the portrait?"

"Yes," came the simple reply.

"Now you flatter me!" Jennifer said. She shook her head, then faced him again, sadness and longing etched on her face. "I know I'm being foolish. I know she had to have been someone you loved, so I fixed myself up to look even more like her. Do you know why, Paul? I doubt it." She shut her eyes holding back the ache she felt. "It was wrong of me—a 'miscalculation' I'll call it. But then I'm not very experienced in such things, you see."

"Jennifer, whatever are you talking about?"

She studied his gray eyes and couldn't speak. She took a few steps backwards, away from him, as if she needed to increase the distance before any words came to her. Finally words came. "You and I, that's what this is about. Or should I say, you and that woman. You loved her in your life, and I believe you still do. The only reason you tolerate me at all is because I remind you of her. But not enough. I'm not her, after all, am I?"

"So that's it," Paul looked at her. He stood and walked towards her. "You foolish child. Her name was Amelia. I did love her, and I always will, but that was long ago." He stood close, and looked into her eyes. "I will admit that at first I tolerated you because you reminded me of her, but then I came to know Jennifer. Do you really think I spent so many evenings talking to you and enjoying your company simply because you resemble someone else? I enjoy your company for you, yourself. I don't care who you look like."

"Really?" she asked.

"Really!" he laughed.

"I wish I could have known you then," Jennifer whispered.

"Then?" Paul didn't understand.

"When you were alive, and alone. I would

have tried to make you forget Amelia! Clearly it didn't work out for you." Her voice turned harsh, bitter. "I would have done all I could to help you enjoy the life you had, not regret what could not be."

"And what about you, Jennifer? Are you enjoying the life you have? Or are you filled with regrets?"

"I didn't enjoy very much it before, I'll admit. I always felt as if something—someone—was missing. I never knew what…until now. Now, with you…."

"Jenny?" Sue's voice called out. Jennifer heard Sue's footsteps coming down the stairs. She looked at Paul, what was he going to do? He turned and sat in the leather chair, looking calm and collected.

She was quite the opposite, and wondered if Sue would be aware of his presence in any way.

"Jenny, is everything all right?" Sue stopped in the doorway. She stepped into the room and looked from Jennifer to the leather chair. "Am I interrupting something?"

"Everything is fine," said Jennifer as she crossed the room to sit at the window seat. *Sue can't see him!* Her breathe quickened. Was he real? Was she going mad? "I'm okay. I was just, um, just trying to memorize some lines from a play the school district is going to put on. I thought I might try out for a part."

Sue looked at her incredulously, and appeared increasingly awkward stand there. Finally she said, "I guess I'll get back upstairs. I'm sorry to have bothered you and your friend, Jenny." At that Sue nodded at Paul and left the room.

Jennifer could hardly believe her ears. "Paul," she ran to him, but stopped just short of reaching where he sat. "She saw you!"

"Of course. I decided to let her." He smiled. "You foolish girl! Did you still think I was a figment of your imagination? After all this time? I'm real; as real as anything in this world, in fact."

"I can hardly believe it. Oh Paul, I'm so glad."

He laughed. "You didn't really believe that unimaginative mind of yours could conjure up someone of my knowledge and abilities?"

She couldn't help but join his laughter. "You are the least humble person I've ever met!" To her horror, tears inexplicably filled her eyes.

"Well, the idea of being nothing more than a figment of another's mind is hardly flattering." He stopped speaking, then abruptly stood. "You aren't crying are you?"

"No! At least, I don't think so." She quickly wiped the tears from her cheeks. "Don't argue with me. Don't chide me, please Paul, not tonight of all nights."

"Jennifer," he whispered, his voice filled with kindness as he stepped closer, too close.

Her blue eyes searched his face, and then met and locked with his soft gray ones. It seemed an eternity that she regarded him, not speaking and not moving for fear of breaking the spell, of disrupting the magic she found in him that moment. For that moment, she felt she looked into his soul, and found a warmth and closeness she never before found in another person.

But then, as if the spell must be broken, he lowered his gaze and walked away from her. He stopped at the window, staring out at the blackness of the night outside. "I don't mean to chide you, Jennifer. Not really. It's just my way."

"I know."

"There's so much...so much I wish you did understand..."

"You can explain it to me."

"No...there's nothing I can say, Jennifer. It's feeling—the feeling explains it, you see. I see you with your friends, young men who can offer you so much. I envy them."

"I'm happy with you."

He faced her once more, his expression sad, tortured. "I wonder if you'll feel that way tomorrow, or the day after, or the day after that."

"Of course I will! I'll never change—there's no way I would!"

Paul dropped his gaze and she felt as if she had watched something beautiful, like the gateway to a palace open and reveal its splendor, and then close again as he withdrew. "Paul..." she cried, wanting to bring him back, emotionally, to her once more.

"It's late, Jennifer. You probably should get some sleep."

"How can I sleep? You make me feel you want to leave me."

"My foolish one," Paul looked at her tenderly. "I'll be here. I'll always be here. It's you, you see, who should have a choice....But aside from that, I really must not see you for the few days your friends are here. We should have no more surprises such as Sue offered us."

"Come back to me soon!"

"I'll be nearby," Paul said as he turned to leave the room.

"Paul!" Jennifer took two steps in his direction and held out her hand. It was a small gesture; one that would have been all but insignificant for most people, yet, as she did it she realized she had never touched Paul. And so she reached her hand out to him, and waited.

She recognized that Paul understood the significance of her gesture, the pounding anticipation in her heart. He, more than anyone, ever, understood her moods, feelings and anxieties, perhaps even more than she realized.

As her hand remained steady, he reached toward it. Slowly, their hands came closer, their fingertips touched, then intertwined and held. He raised his free hand to her face, lightly ran it along her cheek, over her hair, then fingered a curl by her ear. "It's been more than a century since I touched another person," he whispered, his voice filled with awe and even a little reverence. "You're soft. Like heaven."

Then he dropped his hands and stepped back from her, his gaze sadder than she had ever seen it. He quickly turned and left the room as softly and unobtrusively as he had entered it.

Jennifer watched, fingers pressed to her lips. His touch was the most wonderful, yet the most puzzling sensation she had ever felt. It was warm and strong, like the touch of any man, but yet, it was as if Jennifer's hand and face had been caressed by the wind. She stood without moving, elated and saddened at the same time. She loved him.

She loved Paul Squire and that meant…what?

Chapter 17

JENNIFER BARELY SLEPT that night, her mind kept racing over words Paul had spoken. In her dream he was an affectionate and loving man— alive and warm. She woke up troubled by the difference between the dream and reality, and then laughed as she thought of Paul and reality in one mind. But what was reality if not Paul?

Downstairs, she made a pot of coffee, then took a cup outside. It was another beautiful morning. Beau and Jock romped boisterously. The songs of the last birds of autumn filled the woods in counter rhythm with the caws of the seagulls making their morning catches over the ocean and then swooping inland to brag of their achievements.

Jennifer leaned back against a tree facing the sea, enjoying the sounds of morning when she heard approaching footsteps. She peered over her shoulder to see Brent, a cup of steaming coffee in hand.

"Good morning," he said as he sat down beside

her.

"Good morning. I thought I was the only one crazy enough to be up so early," she said.

"I smelled the coffee in my sleep. It lured me right out of bed. Also I had to see the bewitching creature who could prepare such an enticing brew."

"You are so full of the blarney!"

"As a matter of fact, I am part Irish. Scottish too. I guess that's why I've got so much inner turmoil. The Scots and the Irish rarely agree on anything."

"So I've heard," she said with a smile.

"How about you? What's your background?" Brent asked.

"It's a lucky person who knows his ethnicity. I don't know. 'Heinz 57' I guess."

"Well I know: half wood-nymph and half sphinx." He leaned toward her and took her hand. "A sprite, not part of this earth."

She pulled her hand back. "Sometimes I think I'm too much of this earth, my friend." She stood, uncomfortable about the way this conversation was going.

"Walk with me, please?" Brent asked. "It's

beautiful out here!"

She couldn't help but agree. They headed towards a craggy knoll about a half mile from the house, Beau and Jock at their heels. It was an easy climb to the knoll, and the brisk morning air refreshed and exhilarated them. From there, miles of coastline were bright and glorious in the morning sun.

Brent leapt up on one of the huge boulders half buried on the landscape. "I'm king of the mountain!" he shouted.

"You look like him, too!" she called. She found a place to sit where she could enjoy the view. After a while Brent came down and joined her.

He spoke, "I wonder if the natives realize what a fine spot they live in?"

"The natives?"

"I didn't mean it that way. You know what I did mean. You understand me quite a bit I think, Jennifer, much more than you like to let on."

"Are you so enigmatic, Brent?" Jennifer asked.

"I wouldn't have thought so, but you'd be surprised at how others see me. All except you."

"I'm nothing special. Don't think that I am."

"You're wrong, Jennifer. From the moment I met you I knew it."

Jennifer didn't like the way he was talking to her. "I hate to tell you this, but the moment I met you, I didn't like you."

"Oh....Maybe that was the something special I felt!" He looked so stunned, Jennifer couldn't help but chuckle.

"Why did you dislike me?" he asked. "I know I was tired from the long drive but I didn't think I acted that much the ogre."

She wished she hadn't spoken. How could she tell him it was his treatment of Sue that had formed her opinion? "I guess I'm just such a solitary soul that I flash hostile to anyone disturbing that. Don't take it personally, really. I shouldn't have said anything."

Brent looked at her sadly, or at least with as much sadness as the large blue eyes, fantastic tan and flashing white teeth could muster. Jennifer wondered if she were being overly critical of him because of, rather than in spite of, his good looks. "Do you still feel that way?"

Jennifer felt herself mellow. "Not really."

"I'm glad," Brent gave her one of those dazzling smiles that could melt the heart of stronger stuff than Jennifer was made of. She felt herself blushing, and quickly diverted her gaze to the hillside.

"Jenny," Brent said taking her hand once more. "You're right out of mythology, like a fairy princess, and all this is your kingdom, the land of the realm."

And again she quickly took back her hand. "Why do you say such things to me?"

"Because," he said, tapping the end of her nose with one finger, "I've never met anyone like you. You have such independence here. This place, you…it's not the world as I know it, but as I would like it to be."

She looked out at the valley. "You're an idealist, Brent. But the world isn't ideal."

"It can be…near you," he whispered.

She could feel his gaze on her, waiting for her reaction to his last statement.

She stood. "You're wrong, Brent. Completely wrong. I'm going back."

As she started to stand, he clutched her arm,

stopping her. "Don't hide from me, please. I think, in you, I've finally met someone with whom I can be myself—no pretense, no airs. You know what I'm saying. I know you understand."

She pulled her arm free, disgust and anger etching her face. "How can you talk that way to me? How can you forget Sue, my best friend. She's like a sister to me, and she loves you! Has she given her heart to someone who cares so little? How many other women have you talked to like this while with her? How can you, with all your talk of understanding and putting aside pretense, be so false with my friend?"

"It's not what you think." He placed his hands on her shoulders. "To answer your question, I have never spoken this way to another woman, not since I met Sue, and not even before I knew her. Do you know why? It's because I never felt like this before. Sue knows our relationship isn't what it should be. We've been close, more than close, but we're not in love. Ask her yourself if you don't believe me! We've become friends, friends with benefits I suppose the kids would say, but nothing more. A part of me will always care deeply about her, but it's a comfortable love, and I'm not a comfortable person. I need more. Sue knows that. She knows she and I *both* deserve a lot more than we give each other. "

"That's not how she sees it."

"Are you sure about that?"

She hated to admit the truth to his words; she had felt it when Sue spoke of him, she had seen it when she watched the two of them together. "Perhaps the right kind of love will grow between you given more time?"

"Do you think it happens that way between people? Don't you think there's usually some magic first?"

She stepped aside, breaking his hold. "Maybe magic in love doesn't exist. It's something poets have invented, or high school kids out on prom night."

She turned and headed back to her house, but had only gone a few steps when Brent caught up and took her arm, stopping her progress. "You don't really believe that, you know." He turned her towards him and placed his hands on her slender waist. "You're too much like me, an idealist and a dreamer."

She put her hands on his chest to hold him back. "You're so wrong."

"I'm not," he whispered as he leaned closer and gently kissed her. She pulled back, stunned. Yet it had been so long since she'd been kissed, she couldn't stop the quickening of her heartbeat, couldn't ignore the sudden longing for a man's touch.

"It's impossible!" She spun away from him and ran back towards Squire House. Her bouviers followed her, looking warily at Brent and this strange turn of events.

As Jennifer climbed over the fence she saw that Ross had already arrived. She slowed her pace considerably, but was still warm and flushed.

"Hi," Ross called. "Did you go for a walk or something?"

"Yes," Jennifer said as she approached him, trying to catch her breath.

"Are you all right?" he asked, hardly able to miss the redness of her cheeks and her agitated state.

"Yes, yes," she said, and then her eye caught

the two coffee cups sitting on the stump of a tree not ten feet from where Ross stood. He must have seen them, Jennifer thought, so after a lengthy pause she added, "Oh, and Brent also decided to take a walk." She waved her arm about awkwardly. "He's out there somewhere still, I guess."

"Right."

Jennifer couldn't help but suspect he guessed more than she would have hoped.

Sue was in the kitchen when they entered. "Finally!" she exclaimed. "I was afraid I'd been deserted. I got up and the house was completely empty. They say country folk are up with the chickens. Now, I believe it!"

"Good morning." Jennifer felt horribly self-conscious. "I went out for a walk. So did Brent. I'm sure he'll return soon."

The three sat around the kitchen table and talked as they had so many months ago when they first met. They joked and kidded, and enjoyed the nonsense they spoke of. They hadn't had the opportunity at the Thanksgiving dinner to bring back the camaraderie they had once shared.

Brent eventually returned to Squire House. Sue

warmly offered to cook him some breakfast. Jennifer tried to act nonchalant, but she felt stiff and awkward. Ross was close to hostile and treated Brent as nothing more than an intruder in their midst.

The four soon piled into Ross' car to journey to Clevewick. The trip took them about ten miles north along the coast highway. Part of the Clevewick land bordered Highway 1, and it was there that the dairy goods processing plant was located.

Ross turned off the highway onto a narrow road that led to an entrance with stone posts on either side and a metal archway with the name Clevewick. Past the entrance the drive continued for three-quarters of a mile through redwoods until they reached a wide clearing. In the center stood a palatial home, three stories tall and over a hundred feet wide.

Ross drove up to the front of the house and stopped the car. Everyone got out. Sue was concerned about him leaving his clunker in the driveway, but he laughed assured her it was perfectly all right.

When they entered the house, Sue and Jennifer gaped in surprise at the elegance around them. The entry hall was easily the size of Jennifer's living room. A small oriental carpet lay on the floor with an elaborate chandelier over it, an antique table and mirror stood against one wall, and two Chippendale chairs at another. But the focal point was a large curved staircase, the type that commanded a royal entrance for anyone descending it.

"Come with me," Ross said. "I'd like you to meet my mother."

Ross showed them into a large room at the end of the hall. "Mother?" he said, "I've brought friends."

Jennifer and Sue later agreed that they were not sure which impressed them most upon first stepping into that room—the grand room itself, or the petite, frail woman dressed in black, sitting on a chesterfield amidst a plethora of pillows propped up to hold her in an upright position.

Jennifer, Sue and Brent stepped into the room and huddled in the doorway.

"Come in, come right in and sit down, please," said Mrs. Alderworth in a voice barely above a whisper.

Ross reached over and took Jennifer's arm and led her towards his mother. Sue and Brent followed as if the three were chained together.

"Mother," Ross began, "I'd like you to meet Jennifer Barrett, Susan Sanderville and Brent Cooper." Then turning to his friends, he presented his mother.

They greeted each other with assorted pleasantries, and finally Ross succeeded in getting the three to take seats.

Mrs. Alderworth studied Jennifer for a while in silence, then she spoke, "I understand you are living in Squire House alone. Is it to your liking?"

"Very much so," Jennifer responded. "It's a beautiful house."

"Do you like our small town?" Mrs. Alderworth continued.

"Oh, yes. Everyone has been kind to me."

Mrs. Alderworth nodded in agreement then turned her attention to Sue, seeming to make a special study of Sue before speaking. "And you, Miss Sanderville, do you like Brynstol?"

Sue was hardly expecting this question, but

answered by saying, "Please call me Sue, Mrs. Alderworth. I think, as Jennifer does, that Brynstol is quite lovely."

"How does life here compare to San Francisco?" the older woman asked Sue again.

"Probably in no way at all," Sue said, then turned to Jennifer who smiled and nodded in agreement. But then, Sue became serious, "The two places could be in two different worlds. Each has its good points, and each its bad. It depends on how an individual wants to live that would determine which he or she prefers, I think."

"It's been a long time since I was in San Francisco," Mrs. Alderworth said. "I was very young then. Mr. Alderworth took me. I'd been in big cities before, but I was born and raised in a little town called Occidental. Nothing but a post office station marked where the farms ended and the town began.

"My parents decided I should go to Brown University on the East Coast—to get the sort of education that would allow me to do more than live on a dairy farm if I wished. I didn't care for the East Coast, however. I found it all too busy and too depressing. So, when I met Mr. Alderworth, who was just starting to buy some land to try to make a go of his farm, I was ready to help." She pursed her lips. "But I digress. Forgive an old woman! Anyway, Mr. Alderworth brought me to San Francisco many times. What fun we had! We went to nightclubs and danced the night away." She smiled at the memory, and her eyes took on a sparkle they had lacked until that moment. "My lady friends around here considered that quite scandalous!"

The women laughed a bit with Mrs. Alderworth over this little tale, but Brent became very serious.

He spoke, "Excuse me, Mrs. Alderworth." She turned towards this handsome young man that she had, in fact, rather ignored up to this point. "You mentioned that Mr. Alderworth was starting to build a farm. This isn't the farm he built, is it?"

"I should say it is!" she exclaimed.

"Then Ross isn't a hired hand?" Brent blurted out.

Mrs. Alderworth looked at Ross, and he at her with equal astonishment. "Ross, what have you been telling these people?" Mrs. Alderworth asked.

"I haven't said any such thing!" He looked at Sue and Jennifer in surprise.

The two were embarrassed by Brent's remarks. They realized their mistake just by observing Ross' manner as he lead them through the house. He walked as an owner, not an employee.

Sue mumbled, "Well, when you said something about work, we just assumed, I guess, that the owners of all this wouldn't have to work, I mean…you know?"

Ross grinned at her.

Mrs. Alderworth spoke up, "It was, perhaps, a natural mistake my dears. So many young people these days don't work for what they have. But then, I believe that unless one works for something it isn't fully appreciated. My husband and I worked for this land. We worked long, hard hours in the beginning. Very long hours! As people began to come to this area there was no big farm or dairy available to support them. So as the need for our products grew, we grew to meet the demand."

"And the name Clevewick?" asked Sue, "We suspected the Clevewick family owned this land."

"Ah yes, that does cause people to wonder," continued Mrs. Alderworth. "My husband was born and raised in Clevewick, England. He left his family and moved to this country. He traveled to San Francisco where he got a job as a salesman— apparently women loved his accent!—and began saving money and exploring the area. When he came to Brynstol it reminded him of the Cornish coast of England, where Clevewick is located. It's a harsh land, but he learned as a boy how to work in this type of countryside and climate. So after about ten years of work and saving he was finally able to realize his dream and he bought a small piece of this land and put up a small house. He nearly starved that first winter, as you can imagine. But slowly things got better. By the time we married another ten years had passed for him. (I was just a young thing, then, I might add.)

"Our son—we were only blessed with one child—worked right alongside his father through many a severe storm in winter or drought in summer. Isn't that right, Ross?"

"It is. It wasn't bad, though, looking back," added Ross.

"How true. Wait until you're my age—the farther back you look the rosier life seems. There must be some theorem or law to that effect, isn't there, Mr. Cooper?" she turned her gaze again at Brent.

"If there isn't, I'm sure there should be," he said.

"Let's make one then," said Sue. "We'll call it Alderworth's Law. How about, 'Life enhances in geometrical proportion to its distance from the current date.'"

"I like that!" the older woman said with a laugh. "Very impressive."

Ross stood. "Well friends, I hope you're ready to take a look at the dairy here. That's what we came for."

Sue, Jennifer and Brent stood, and thanked Mrs. Alderworth for her hospitality. She told them they would be welcome in her house anytime.

The dairy was a large operation with machinery doing much of the work that dairymen did in the past. Still, there was need for a number of people to take care of the animals, another group to see that the machinery worked properly, and another for quality control. At one time or another Ross had learned every job on the farm. Only in that way, he felt, could he know how well or how poorly the whole operation was functioning.

In the middle of the tour, one of the house servants brought them a picnic basket Ross' mother had ordered prepared. It was full of treats—southern-fried chicken, paté, roast beef sandwiches on San Francisco sour dough bread, Mandarin oranges, walnuts, two bottles of Perrier and one of merlot from the Napa valley.

After a leisurely lunch the group finished touring Clevewick and decided to spend the rest of the afternoon on the beach.

Two fishermen were busy at work hoping to catch some sea bass. They had a little black and white dog that ran around in circles near the men, as if to inspire them in their work.

Another man and his little son appeared almost out of nowhere and walked along the beach. He waved at the group huddled over the fire as he and the boy passed by. Other than that the beach and surrounding areas were completely devoid of any indication that man existed or had any hand in affecting nature or the environment.

It wasn't warm on the beach. The winter wind carried a piercing bite, but everyone was dressed warmly, and Ross and Brent built a warm bonfire.

As the day wore on the beach became too chilly for comfort, even with the bonfire. So the small company decided to spend the rest of the evening down the coast some twenty miles at the Blue Rock Café, a popular seafood restaurant and bar. Since this was a Friday, a small dance band played.

Each of the four was in excellent spirits. Jennifer was glad that when Brent asked her to dance he made no mention of what had passed between them that very morning. She hoped it would be forgotten. Yet, the way he held her close, and the way she felt by his nearness, she knew that although their kiss was not spoken of, it was not forgotten either.

Jennifer was glad to see Sue and Ross dance together often and that Sue seemed quite happy with Ross. The events of the day confirmed her opinion that Brent wasn't the right person for Sue. She could only hope that when Sue came to that realization, she wouldn't be hurt by it.

Ross' obvious feelings for Sue also helped clarify his relationship with Jennifer. She could now relax with him, and he with her, on a strictly friendly basis, with no overtones to cloud their enjoyment of each other's company.

By the time they arrived back at Squire House it was quite late, so Ross left immediately and Jennifer, Brent and Sue retired for the night.

A short while after Jennifer was in bed she heard a light knocking on her door. She sat up and lit the lamp by her bed. The tapping began again.

"Are you awake, Jenny?" It was Sue. Jennifer hadn't realized she had been holding her breath until she heard it come out in a sigh of relief.

"Yes, I'm awake, come in," she called.

Sue entered the room and quietly shut the door behind her, then sat at the foot of Jennifer's bed. "You'll think I'm incredibly nosy, and I'd say you're right, but I couldn't sleep another night without knowing who that strange man was that I saw you with last night."

Here it was at last, Jennifer thought. She suspected the question would be asked, and she had even prepared an answer, but somehow the entire episode from last night seemed like a dream instead of reality, and in the light of day she couldn't bring herself to give it any serious consideration. Now, faced with the question, she remained mute, knowing she had to lie to Sue, but finding it difficult nonetheless.

"Won't you tell me?" Sue asked again, sounding rather hurt. "I guess I really shouldn't have asked. If you wanted to tell me, you would have, or at least introduced me to him. It's just that when I entered the room and saw how you two looked at each other....He's really special to you, isn't he? I've never seen you look at a man like that before. So, anyway, I thought you might want to talk about him. But if not, that's okay. Just know I'm here, and available…if you want to talk, as I said…" Sue stopped and waited expectantly for a reply.

Jennifer had to smile. "You caught me by surprise, first last night and then again tonight by your question."

"Oh?" Sue didn't actually say the words "please continue," but they were implicit in her tone.

"I don't really know what to say about him."

Sue was silent, waiting.

"You're right. He is special to me. He's an artist, a painter, a very good one, too. Maybe someday he'll be famous."

"Is he as good as your Paul Squire?" Sue asked.

"I would say he's quite the equal."

"Can I see some of his work?"

Jennifer thought a moment. "Probably not. Well, perhaps someday," she added, not wanting to make too much of a mystery about this.

Sue was puzzled. "An artist not willing to show his work? What's his name?" she asked.

"Peter." It was the first name that came to Jennifer's mind.

The minute she said it she regretted it—Peter and Paul were so joined in her own mind she couldn't say one name without conjuring the other. She looked at Sue quizzically. Had the same thought flashed into her mind? But Sue showed no sign of anything but blanket acceptance of what Jennifer was saying, causing Jennifer to wonder what kind of look Sue would wear if she learned the truth.

"He's special to you, but you didn't invite him to your dinner?"

"It…it's complicated. He's a loner, Sue. It's really impossible to explain." *Finally, the truth!* Jennifer thought.

"Where does he live?" Sue asked.

"I'm not sure."

"How does he live?"

"I don't know that either."

"Have you known him very long?"

This was much more difficult than Jennifer had imagined it would be. "Six months." Then, with a sigh she added, "Forever, if one were to judge by how well he seems to understand me."

"I guess he's got an artist's soul," Sue said softly.

"I guess that's it," Jennifer murmured.

"Do you feel you can trust him, Jenny?" Sue asked, unable to hide her worry about this peculiar man.

Jennifer thought about Paul for a while before answering that. "Definitely. I know his moods, and his reactions, and his feelings, but I don't know if I will ever come to know his thoughts. They are quite beyond the scope of knowledge any mere mortal can possess. He's brilliant, and knows much more than anyone I've ever met."

"You're in love with him," Sue said, stunned and awed by this realization.

Jennifer's breath caught. "I don't, I don't know…"

Sue laughed. "I do! Girl, you are so hooked! God, I wish I could meet him!"

Jennifer was completely flustered. "He's gone away for a while. I don't know if he'll ever be back."

"You're kidding me!"

Jennifer shook her head, dropping her gaze to her hands.

"I'm sorry." Sue squeezed her hand. "If I'd known, I wouldn't have said—"

"It's all right," Jennifer whispered. "As I said, it's complicated."

"I hope you find out more about him, though. I mean, hell, he might even be married!" Sue frowned.

"He's not married, Sue. That much I do know. For God's sake, don't worry about me. I know him well enough. I like him, nothing more. There's nothing between us."

"Okay. I'll trust your judgment—but I know you're kind of inexperienced around men..."

"Kind of?" Jennifer laughed at the understatement.

"Well, anyway," Sue continued, standing up, "I'm glad to hear that there's someone up here to warm these cold winter evenings! Speaking of which, I'd better jump back into bed before I freeze. Good night now."

"Good-night," Jennifer responded as Sue dashed out of the room.

She shut the light, but could hear the barely audible tones of Brent's voice as Sue entered the guest room. The guest room door clicked shut, and seconds later Jennifer heard giggles and low outbursts of laughter. She turned over on her side and buried her head deeper into her pillow, trying to muffle out the sounds.

What was going on in Brent's mind, she wondered. This morning, he professed devotion—

or something—to her, and now he was laughing with Sue in his bed. It didn't make sense.

Thank God, it didn't sound as if anything more than talking was going on next door.

She rolled onto her back, feeling very alone in her large bed, and stared at the ceiling.

Did she believe Brent sincerely thought he could be happy with her and Brynstol? Perhaps he was, but she also wondered how long that 'enthusiasm,' to use Sue's word, would last?

She had to admit he was physically attractive. She liked the way he held her when they danced, the way he looked at her as if she were not only special, but beautiful. She wondered if he had looked at Sue that way when they first began to date.

And he was a flesh and blood, a man in need of love and willing to give love in return.

She flung her arm out against the mattress, the cold, empty mattress beside her.

How ironic that for all her life Jennifer had sought love, marriage, a home, children. That was what she believed would make her happy.

But then she met Paul…

She shut her eyes and flopped on her side again, this time away from the emptiness of the bed, towards the side, towards her bed table. But her mind wouldn't give up. It ticked off the options.

Brent was real, like her.

Alive.

Of this life.

Brent—or someone like him—was what she needed. Not a ghost! Was she crazy? A ghost? *Really, Jennifer??*

She would have to forget about Paul. He was ethereal, nothing more. She must put him out of her mind. To do otherwise would be against nature.

Thinking about him, loving him was not only unnatural, it was mentally sick.

The other room had become quiet, and yet Jennifer's mind raced on, not letting her sleep or even rest. She rolled over onto the opposite side of the bed, but still her thoughts continued.

Thoughts of the guest room kept invading her mind. She had to admit it to herself, she wanted love in all senses of the word, and once allowing the thought to be admitted into her mind she physically ached from the admittance of it. She had needs, wants and desires of any normal woman.

Who had ever been interested in her in the past? Some pimply high-school boys that she had refused to dance with; a couple of men from the office whose prime distinguishing features were sweaty palms; and a lonely old realtor. Some string of suitors! Yet, despite them, or because of them, she had been choosy about her heart. She had vowed to keep it her own until she met a man who was just right.

But didn't there come a time when a person must admit that life wasn't perfect? That it wouldn't always turn out like an idealistic school girl's dream? There were compromises one had to make. That's what life was all about.

She had to learn to face it.

Chapter 18

ON SATURDAY, JENNIFER, Sue and Brent went to Cape Mendocino. The scenery was breathtaking. In the town of Mendocino, they visited galleries and ate fresh crab salads. In the evening, Ross came over to Squire House and they played bridge and talked. Brent, Sue and Jennifer were exhausted from the day's excursion so the evening ended early.

Now, on Sunday, Brent and Sue decided to set off early so that they could have a leisurely trip back to the City—Brent had to be at work on Monday, so Sue's initial plans to stay through Tuesday had changed..

They loaded up the car. Sue got in when Brent said he had forgotten his book and then headed for the house asking Jennifer to help him find it.

She followed Brent inside, but once there he led her into the living room and put his arms around her.

"I want you to know I meant every word I said

to you Friday morning," he told her. "Don't forget them. If you can ever find room for me in your heart I'll be waiting. I think I'm falling in love with you, and I don't know what to do about it."

Jennifer had placed her hands on his shoulders. "I do remember what you said, but—"

He cut off her words with a kiss. She sank into it for a moment, then pushed him away as she realized how vulnerable she felt, and how wrong this was. "Let's find that book," she said, stepping away from him.

"I just remembered, I packed it after all," he replied. Then he brushed his hand against her cheek. "Jenny," said whispered and drew her close for another kiss.

"Am I disturbing something?" a man's voice said.

Brent spun around and stood face to face with Paul Squire. "Who are you?" he cried.

Jennifer could hardly believe her eyes. There stood Paul, but as she had never seen him. His eyes blazed in anger at her. She spoke quickly, "Oh, Brent, this is an old friend of mine, Peter. Peter, this is Brent."

Paul gave her a look that could have struck her dead where she stood. He nearly snarled as the words came out. "An *old* friend. Yes, so I am." His eyes never left Jennifer's as he spoke.

Brent looked from one to the other then turned in anger to Paul, "I didn't hear you come in. Are you in the habit of just walking into a lady's house uninvited?"

"Lady, you say? I may not have been as unexpected as you believe, sir," Paul replied with a piercing glare at Brent, "After all, we are such grand *old* friends!"

Brent was speechless, confusion all over his face as he looked from Paul to Jennifer, whose face now flamed red.

"It's not what you think," Jennifer said as she grabbed Brent's arm and pushed him towards the front door. "It's the way country folks are, Brent. The door is always open."

"Country folks!" Paul hooted.

Jennifer tried to ignore this as she led Brent to the door. "I'm sure Sue is wondering what's happening in here."

"I may be in the same state," Brent replied.

They reached the front door. Brent was about to step through the doorway when, instead, he turned around. "Jennifer, I—"

He was suddenly out the door and it slammed shut.

It took a moment before Jennifer was able to open the door again. Brent was halfway to the car. "A sudden draft," she called. "Sorry!"

He looked confused, then nodded, and got in the car. Sue started the motor, and both waved goodbye as she drove away. She was going to drive the first half of the trip home, and Brent the second.

Jennifer stood in the doorway waving goodbye until the car disappeared. She sighed. She suddenly felt very tired and very confused.

Jennifer went back into the living room expecting to see Paul, but he wasn't there. She sat down in the big leather chair that Paul so loved and watched the seagulls playing over the ocean.

Chapter 19

JENNIFER SPENT THE next week alone. She desperately missed Paul, but at the same time understood why he was staying away. She left out glasses of sherry and even some new pipe tobacco as a peace offering, but each morning she found everything just as she had left it the night before.

She invited Ross to dinner on Saturday night, and happily he accepted. Jennifer felt quite lonely all week after the excitement of having had so much company. Also, she was sure Ross would want to talk to her about Sue, and on that score, she felt that the sooner something positive happened the better it would be for all concerned.

He arrived at five o'clock on the dot. It was already dark out. Winter nights came quickly to the north coast communities. Ross brought some fancy French pastries for dessert, made by his family cook with lots of cream and butter as befitting a dessert from a dairyman. Jennifer was quite pleased by the present, as she had always been fond of fancy desserts.

"What have you been up to all week?" Jennifer asked Ross when they settled down in the living room for some pre-dinner conversation.

"Nothing much. Same old stuff with the dairy. It was, luckily, a pretty quiet week. I found I wasn't too much into the business last week."

"Because of Sue?" Jennifer asked.

"I can't get her out of my mind." Ross slumped back in his chair and looked to Jennifer almost like a parody of every unhappy lover the world has ever known.

Jennifer smiled at him, "But why should you even want to get her out of your mind? It would seem that thoughts of Sue would make you happy."

Ross snorted, "Oh, Sue makes me happy. It's just that when I think of her I also see the playboy of the Western world. And don't think I didn't notice how he was mooning around after you right under her nose! She should have thrown the bum out of here."

"Maybe I should have," sighed Jennifer.

"Maybe so!" Ross agreed, but then he began to think about it a bit more. "No, maybe not. That would have caused quite a scene. And then, maybe Sue didn't notice anything. But she must have, don't you think?"

"I'm sure she noticed something. But then, she's known Brent a long time. Maybe he's just that way and she accepts it."

"Why should she settle for a guy like that?"

"Why do any of us do anything, Ross?" Jennifer asked rhetorically. "Maybe she thinks he'll improve. Maybe she's just tired and the effort of leaving would be too much trouble. Maybe she's lonely and needs someone to pass the hours with. Or, most likely, she knows he's not the right man for her and so she simply doesn't much care."

At that, he perked up. "You think?"

"Sue and I used to spend a lot of time together. I'm the type that doesn't mind being alone, I often enjoy it in fact. But Sue isn't that way. She needs companionship. With Brent she has that. I don't think he's a bad person—just confused and unsure of what he wants or how to get it."

"But Sue could have any man she chooses. Why isn't she with someone that she seems happier with?"

Jennifer had to smile at this outburst. "You are a goose, Ross Alderworth! First of all, it's not that easy to meet the right person. You should know that. After all, you're not attached, not even a steady girlfriend. Yet you, if you'll excuse my saying so, would be a fine catch! You're good looking, witty, pleasant to be around, well-educated and have money besides. So don't go around saying that 'Miss' Right is easy to find when you know from your own experience that isn't so."

"I guess," he admitted somewhat sheepishly.

"And another thing, you wouldn't be saying any of this unless you believed Sue was the right woman for you. Now, if you do feel that way why, in heaven's name, aren't you telling her?"

"Oh, yeah, right!" Ross stood up and walked to the mantelpiece. He ran his fingers through his hair several times and looked completely agitated. "And then I can watch her laugh at me. At least now we can be friends. I can be there if she needs me."

"If she needs you?" asked Jennifer.

"At least I have that. If I say more to her and she rejects me, then what?" Ross pleaded.

"What if you say more and she doesn't reject

you? Why not give her that chance?"

"A chance, you say? What about me, what kind of a chance do you really think I have? Look at that guy Brent. He's on TV! We both have money, but he's also got looks, polish, panache. Compared to him I'm a country bumpkin."

"Sue doesn't think that! Nor do I. Nor do you, for that matter! You're just feeling sorry for yourself and making excuses."

"I'm not."

"Ross Alderworth of Clevewick,"—Jennifer folded her arms—"you're scared to face her."

He took a deep breath. "Maybe so, but she's special to me. And she's already got someone who is special to her. So here I am. Enough said."

"Not quite. Let me say one last thing," Jennifer insisted. "I have seen Sue with Brent and I've seen her with you. I have talked to Sue about how she feels towards Brent, and to him about how he feels about her. In my opinion you have every chance in the world if you go about it the right way."

Finally, hope brightened his face. "Really?"

She nodded.

"What should I do?" he asked.

"I don't know," she said. "But I somehow think if anyone can figure it out, you will."

"You're a doll!"

"Good. In that case, can we eat now?"

As they dined they talked about less weighty subjects than love, although the topic often turned to Jennifer's girlhood where, of course, Sue played a big part.

Chapter 20

THE FOLLOWING WEEKEND Gresham Innes was invited to dine at Squire House. The main topic of conversation that night was Ross Alderworth's sudden departure for San Francisco. There was much speculation in town about Ross' reasons for going. Innes suspected the real reason, but he would have considered it a breaking of trust with Jennifer if he told anyone about Sue, so he did not.

Jennifer was quite sure Ross' going was a result of their conversation. She could only hope that she had said the right thing. It was only a matter of time before Sue and Brent went their separate ways. Why shouldn't Ross, a good man, be there to help the inevitable?

The days passed into weeks and the weeks into months. Christmas came and went very quietly in the house on the hill. Mrs. Petris invited Jennifer and Innes both to her house for a Christmas dinner. Mrs. Petris was a terrible cook, and Innes joked all the way back to Squire House about what brand of dog food he and Jennifer had dined on.

In early February, Jennifer was surprised to receive an invitation to visit Clevewick from Mrs. Alderworth. Ross was still in San Francisco and Jennifer was sure that that was why she had been summoned. She was rather wary of going as she feared it would not be a pleasant experience.

Mrs. Alderworth sent a car to pick her up. Jennifer sat in the back seat, in silence, during the brief ride. When she arrived at the main house she was let into a small side room, not the big room as previously. Tea and pastries were on the table, and a moment later Mrs. Alderworth joined her.

"Forgive an old woman her loss of punctuality," Mrs. Alderworth began.

Jennifer hardly knew how to respond. "Not at all."

Mrs. Alderworth reached a stiff-looking armchair with a high back, and slowly lowered herself into it. She sighed from the effort and shut her eyes briefly. She appeared thinner and frailer than she had when Jennifer first met her.

"I'm glad you accepted my invitation, my

dear," Mrs. Alderworth said. "I had hoped that you might have some information for me."

"I'm not sure what you mean," Jennifer replied.

Mrs. Alderworth looked as if she really didn't want to talk about it, but then said, "Since Ross left, I've only heard from him a few times, and without any detail. I know why he left, and, at the time I approved." She swallowed hard, as if this conversation was difficult for her. "I told him, *'If you love her, son, go find her and tell her so.'* But now—I don't understand it. What went wrong? Have you had any word, Jennifer?"

Jennifer had expected this would be the question asked. "I don't know what to tell you," she said. "I also haven't heard much. Sue has been unusually silent. I know that when Ross first arrived in San Francisco she was upset. But don't be alarmed. This is natural for Sue. She's a very loyal person. She had been seeing Brent for well over six months, and had convinced herself she was in love with him. Then, when Ross showed up, he confused everything. I know she likes him a lot, and if Brent weren't in the picture, I doubt there would be any question in her mind about seeing Ross."

Mrs. Alderworth nodded thoughtfully. "And what about Ross? Have you heard from my son?"

She shook her head. "Other than a Christmas card saying he was seeing Sue quite a bit, and hoped her misplaced loyalty to Brent was wearing thin, no. I've heard nothing."

She didn't speak of the cards, letters, emails, and weekly bouquet of flowers she received from Brent which indicated that Sue's loyalty was, in fact, truly misplaced. They all ended with the words, "Always— Love, Brent."

The frail woman folded her hands, her narrow shoulders square, her back straight. "So perhaps there is hope yet for my son's happiness? He has never done anything like this before. He has always been so level-headed, so practical. Clevewick came first, no matter what. I just don't understand young people anymore. If he does win Sue's love, then what? Will she be happy at Clevewick or will I lose my son forever?"

Jennifer had wondered about this herself. Could Sue live at Clevewick? She had no idea, and answered Mrs. Alderworth frankly.

"What more can I say?" Mrs. Alderworth lowered her head and breathing deeply with emotion, stared at the floor to compose herself. "I will have to remain quietly here in my chair and wait. I haven't much more time to wait, I'm afraid. I'm so tired these days. I had hoped to see my son with a wife—maybe even grandchildren—happy in this home that gave me and my husband such joy. With Ross' love of Clevewick I never considered for a moment that the future would hold any other possibility for this dear house. How ironic that the one thing that I found to be so certain is the thing that now perhaps never shall be."

"I'm sorry," Jennifer murmured.

"Life is very strange, Jennifer. It has curves and twists in it that Solomon with all his wisdom could not understand." She took a moment to catch her breath before adding, "I always taught Ross to follow his heart. I guess I taught him too well." She feebly laughed at her attempt at a joke.

Jennifer ached for the sick, unhappy woman before her. "Ross will work things out best for all the people he loves, and the home he is so proud of.

I'm sure of that. Trust him."

"Thank you." Mrs. Alderworth took Jennifer's hand in her thin one. "I wish it were you Ross fell in love with. What fun we'd have dancing at your wedding!"

Jennifer blushed and could not think of a thing to say.

Mrs. Alderworth spoke again. "I'm afraid I must take my nap now—doctor 's orders. Please let me know immediately if you hear any further news of Ross."

Jennifer promised, and took her leave of Mrs. Alderworth. The chauffeur was waiting to take her back to Squire House.

oOo

Before long it was March, an entire year had passed since Jennifer first came to Brynstol. How different her life had been this year from her prior existence. She was almost happy, but not quite. She loved her house, her dogs, her new friends. She didn't have much money, and had to be exceptionally frugal, but she did not want for anything either. There was just one flaw in the way of life she had found for herself. Paul Squire no longer shared it with her.

The night he saw her and Brent together was the last time she saw him. She remembered the look on his face as she made one false remark after another about him to Brent. She had all but told him that she was in love with him days earlier, and then he saw her kissing Brent and acting as if she had forgotten about him completely. He had misconstrued everything. With his Victorian attitudes, Jennifer was sure the harmlessness with which she regarded Brent's attentions that day were probably not at all the way Paul regarded them.

She tried many times to make peace with him. She literally begged his forgiveness and asked that he come back to Squire House to be with her, but he did not. The first and second weeks of Paul's departure Jennifer could accept. It was not the first time he had gone away in anger from her, but he had always returned. The third week she began to worry, and by the fourth week she had given up hope.

The ghost of Squire House was gone, she thought, back to that unpeaceful rest which he had shunned for so many years. The house was plain now, like any other old house along the coast that had had an interesting, even colorful past, but now was falling into mediocrity and one day into oblivion.

Jennifer felt that her life was the same. She loved Brynstol, she truly did. People were kind. Several of the town's women invited her to their homes, to their book club meetings, and she returned the invitations, but it wasn't enough.

The quietness of her life was finally interrupted one evening in April when Jock and Beau started putting up a terrible ruckus and ran to the front door, barking and bounding around and scratching at the door as if to try to open it.

Jennifer put down the sweater she had been knitting and ran to see what was happening. She quieted the dogs and opened the door just in time to see Sue and Ross coming up the front steps.

"What is this?" she cried in astonishment.

Sue ran up to her and kissed her cheek and Ross did the same. Jennifer looked from one to the other as they stood literally beaming with happiness at her. She suspected what had happened, but waited for one of the two to say the words. Finally Sue did. "We got married."

At that Jennifer grabbed Sue and hugged her and all the while told her how very happy and glad she was to hear such good news. Then she hugged Ross and said the same.

"Come inside," Jennifer said. "We'll have a toast for the bride and groom, and then you two must tell me all about what happened."

Jock and Beau remembered Sue and Ross and did their part greeting the two—almost acting as if they were giving congratulations as well, while Jennifer brought out sherry for a toast.

"To a long and happy life for you both," Jennifer said holding her glass high. The glasses clinked together as Ross and Sue thanked her.

They sat, and Jennifer asked if they had seen Ross' mother yet.

"Yes," Sue replied. "We telephoned from City Hall in San Francisco last night to tell her the news, and left the city early this morning. We went straight to Clevewick and were there by about one o'clock. Ross' mother was a little miffed, I think, at not getting to give her little boy away in a big church service."

"She'll get over it," Ross said. "Anyway, when I saw her I was glad we decided against a big wedding, the strain might have been too hard on her."

"I hope she'll get better," Jennifer said.

"Probably not..." Ross responded quietly. "Let's just hope she gets no worse for a long, long time."

Jennifer needed to change the tone of the conversation, so said brightly, "But tell me about you two. What happened?"

They looked at each other and laughed. Sue began, "Frankly, I gave up! He came to San Francisco and said he would not go away until I married him. I tried to get rid of him, but he's beyond stubborn. Finally, what could I do? I needed some peace!"

"Seriously now," said Jennifer.

"Seriously, she's right," Ross added. "I went to the city, got a place, and began spending all the time I possibly could with Sue and Brent. Whenever Brent had to be away, I made it a special point to be alone with Sue. Eventually, even when Brent didn't have to be away I got to be alone with

Sue, and, well, this is the result. What more can I say?"

Jennifer looked at Sue. "I'm so glad, Sue. This is right for you, I really feel it is the right thing that you did."

"I know it is," Sue said seriously, and squeezed Ross' hand ever so slightly, but with ever so much love in that gesture. And he looked at her with complete love in his eyes.

The two asked Jennifer how she had fared over these past months, and seemed not terribly surprised when she mentioned that nothing in particular had happened. Sue said that now that she was going to be living at Clevewick that she and Jennifer would be able to have lots of fun together like old times—or almost like old times, she said with a wink in Ross' direction. Jennifer had to laugh at this. Yes, she was glad Sue would be here. Sue had decided that she would not marry Ross unless she were willing to live at Clevewick because she had recognized very early how important it was in his life. When she accepted Ross' proposal, she accepted Clevewick as well. She knew that as a "big city girl" she would have to make a lot of changes in her life, but she was willing and ready to make them.

Before long Sue and Ross rose to leave. They invited Jennifer to dinner at Clevewick the next day, and also said that they were leaving the day after for a quick one week honeymoon in Hawaii before getting back to business and seeing what kind of a shambles Clevewick had fallen into in Ross' absence. He suspected, actually, that nothing much had happened, but he was looking forward to running the dairy again, and he wanted to believe that it needed him.

Jennifer saw the couple off, and turned back into Squire House. For the first time in many weeks she felt there was some happiness in the world.

Chapter 21

JENNIFER WAS PLEASED to find a postcard in her post office box from Sue and Ross. They must have written it when they first arrived in Hawaii, she thought, for her to have received it so promptly. She looked at the sunny beach shown on the postcard, and felt a twinge of envy. Today was cold, the rain a constant, chilling drizzle.

But the weather put no damper on the town's buzzing with news of the eligible Ross Alderworth's sudden marriage. Many people had seen Sue previously with Jennifer, but this turn of events caught them quite by surprise. Jennifer found herself more popular than ever, getting lots of invitations from people who wanted to learn all she knew.

Gresham Innes was elated by the news. He and Jennifer even had their own celebration dinner because of it—since Ross and Sue had already left for Hawaii they could not be invited. Innes was also happy with the change he saw in Jennifer since her friend's arrival. He had been somewhat worried about her as she had been looking very peaked throughout the winter with an almost morbid desire to be alone in Squire House. But now it was spring, and despite the bad weather, Jennifer seemed much happier.

She hurried back into Squire House with Beau and Jock, relieved to be out of the rain, and had just finished drying them off with thick towels, when her telephone began to ring. She jumped at the sound, a decidedly rare occurrence in this area. So rare, in fact, Jennifer often wondered why she had bothered to have the phone installed in the first place.

She picked it up. "Hello?"

"Hello Jennifer," said a voice she didn't recognize.

"Yes?" she inquired.

"It's me, Brent."

She said nothing.

"How are you?" he asked.

Finally, she found her voice. "Fine. And surprised."

He laughed. "You should have known I'd call

you!"

"Should I?"

"You've seen Sue and Ross by now?" he asked.

"Yes." Jennifer wasn't sure what more she should say.

"I'm really glad for Sue," he continued. "She's got a good man there."

Jennifer was relieved to hear Brent say that. "I think so, too," she added.

"Good."

"Yes." Jennifer was at a loss for words—as Brent seemed to be.

"Jennifer?"

"Yes?"

"I've missed you."

"Oh?"

"It's been a long time since I saw you."

"Yes, yes it has," she whispered.

"A lot can change in that amount of time."

"I guess."

"Not much has changed here," he started to say, and then realized that because of Sue a lot, in fact, had changed. "I mean, with me, at least, nothing has changed."

"That's good," Jennifer said.

"And you?"

"What can I say?"

"Do you feel about me as you did then?"

"No."

"Better?"

"Perhaps."

"Because Sue's out of the picture?"

"Yes."

"I'm glad."

"Me, too."

"Jennifer?"

"Yes?"

"Will you come to San Francisco? A visit. A short visit, if that's all the time you can spare. I miss you. I'd like to spend time with you, to get to know you. Just you and me. Is that too much to ask?"

She didn't answer. His words were unexpected.

"Will you come to me, Jennifer?" he asked.

"This is sudden."

"Not for me," he said. "I've thought of little else since we met."

"You hardly know me."

"Would you prefer I come there again?" he asked.

She thought about Paul Squire's reaction last time Brent was there. "No," she said with a sigh. "I don't think that would be a good idea."

"Getting to know each other," he said, "is half the fun of any relationship. The other half is being comfortable with someone because you do know them so well."

"That's true."

"Would you give me a chance, Jennifer?" he asked. "Would you give *us* a chance? It's crazy. I admit it. But that doesn't mean we shouldn't see where all this leads."

She didn't know what to do, or what to say.

He waited.

"I have to think about it," she replied finally.

"I'm not surprised. That's what makes you, you."

It took a moment before she whispered, "Goodbye, Brent."

"Goodbye, Jennifer."

oOo

She stood alone in the big, empty house, the

silence weighing heavily on her. "If you're still here, Paul, why can't I see you? Why won't you speak to me? Why?"

There was nothing, only more silence. She felt smothered by it, by the...aloneness she felt. By the loneliness.

"I can't!" she cried, then put her coat back on, lifted the hood over her head and walked outdoors. Jock and Beau stood to follow. "No, stay here," she said. "No sense you getting cold, wet, and muddy."

She walked to the edge of her property, over the cliff that faced the sea. She didn't know if it was tears on her face or rain. The wind kicked up and she had to hold the hood tight under her chin to stop it from blowing off. She went down the trail a bit, knowing the breeze would be less fierce closer to the beach than it was at the top of the hill.

She had never gone to that particular beach, the one below the cliff upon which Squire House stood. She wasn't sure why, but now for some reason, she wanted to see it.

The trail was steep, but she had seen Ross and Brent take it, as well as her dogs. She knew where it was and slipped and slid her way down. By concentrating on the trail she could keep her mind off Brent's phone call and everything that was wrong with her life.

She reached the beach and walked along it. It was lovely, even in the rain, and she didn't know why she had never bothered to visit it before. As she walked, she breathed deeply, trying to calm herself. She could handle this, she told herself. It wasn't the first time she'd been disappointed in her life, or in herself. She walked faster.

After all, her own mother had told her time and again that she was unlovable, plain, and boring. Rachel, always surrounded by a throng of friends, would point at Jennifer and say she was sure her baby had been switched with 'that one' at birth. The friends would laugh. Jennifer would laugh, too, only because that was better than to let Rachel know how much her words hurt.

She knew Brent didn't care about her. She intrigued him, that's all. When, *if,* he got to know her, he'd become as bored as everyone else she ever knew. Even Paul, even a *ghost,* couldn't tolerate her for more than a couple of months.

Truth be told, she didn't much care for herself.

She sat on the beach facing the water. The sand was wet, she was soaking from the rain, but none of that mattered as she dropped her head in her hands, eyes shut, trying not to think, not to feel so very empty inside.

She wasn't sure how long she sat there when she became aware that the water had reached her shoes. She scrambled up, surprised at how quickly the tide was coming in, driven by the storm. The waves, too, were much higher than before, and crashed against the shore. She needed to get off the beach fast. She looked for a way, but the cliff here was much sheerer than the one closer to Squire House, and no trail scarred it.

A huge wave struck, reaching her knees, nearly knocking her off her feet. She felt it's strong pull as it washed back out to sea.

She tried to run, knowing she had to travel along the beach some distance, but her shoes sunk deep in the wet sand. They felt as if suction was created, holding them tight. She forced herself forward.

A crashing wave swirled around her, this time almost filling the sandy beach. Her nightmare came back to her, the one in which she was a child running on a beach, frightened. She was frightened now. The next wave knocked her over, but as it went out, she reached the trail back to Squire House.

She began to climb it, but the constant downpour had made the rocks and sand slipperier than she expected, and she kept losing her footing, having to hold on with her bare hands, using her knees as well as her feet to hold on and pull herself up.

"Take my hand!" a voice commanded, a voice she had waited long to hear.

She looked up, and he was perched on the trail, one hand holding the low-hanging branch of a pine tree for support, and the other reaching down towards her. She had to climb up only a little farther and then she stretched out her arm trying to reach him. He slid down a bit closer and she felt his hand take hold of hers. He pulled her towards him, and soon they were both at the top of the cliff.

She lay on it, face down, scared and exhausted.

"You little fool!" he said sitting beside her. "Were you trying to drown yourself or what?"

Slowly, she sat up. "I don't know. What do you care?"

"Maybe I should have left you alone out there on that hillside! Some thanks!"

She pushed the hood off her head, the better to look at him. "What are you doing here?"

"Saving you."

"I mean...is that all?"

"All? You're stark raving mad! Let's get you inside before you add pneumonia to your other ailments."

He put his arm around her and helped her to her feet, then walked her into the house.

She refused to take a hot shower or even dry off until he absolutely promised on all that he held true to still be there when she returned. He did.

262 | Joanne Pence

Chapter 22

WHEN JENNIFER CAME BACK downstairs she found the living room warm, with a raging fire in the fireplace and a cup of hot chocolate waiting for her. She sat before the fire to more quickly dry her long hair.

Paul sat in his leather chair, pipe in mouth, glowering at her.

"I guess I should properly thank you," she said.

"No need."

"I'm so glad you're here, Paul, I—"

"No!"

She was shocked by his tone. "But, I—"

"I want you to leave," he said.

She could scarcely speak. "Leave? But why?"

"I know how Brent Cooper feels about you. I've seen the flowers, the notes. You should listen to him. He's what you need. Not me. I've had a life, a love. And she isn't you."

Of course not. Jennifer tried not to let him see

how much his words hurt. "I see. She's the one you call Amelia."

"Yes."

"You've never talked about her. Don't I at least deserve to know who she was?"

"There's no reason to go into all that."

"No reason? There's every reason! It's because of her I'm supposed to go away. Maybe"—she could scarcely speak for the ache in her heart and her feeling of emptiness—"maybe if I understood, I would want to leave."

He didn't answer.

"Please, Paul."

He tamped the tobacco in his pipe. "You may be right. You deserve to know," he said finally. "It's a long story."

"It doesn't matter," she whispered.

He used a match on his pipe tobacco then, his pipe in good order, he began.

"My parents lived in the east, in Boston. They sent me to boarding schools and summer camps as a child, and away to college as an adult. They took next to no interest in me, my ideas, and especially not in my desire to paint. When I finished college I had no wish to return to their home, which I never considered my home. I traveled to Paris. I met several artists using a style that came to be known as impressionism. I understand Monet became the most popular of them, but it was the realism of the subjects of Édouard Manet that most caught my attention."

Jennifer nodded, glad to hear her thoughts about his work confirmed.

"After studying there a couple of years, however, I missed my country and returned, but I headed west to San Francisco. Since my parents were basically pleased with having me away from them they continued my allowance. It was not generous, but it allowed me to devote myself to my work. I had some small critical successes, and sold a few pictures to men of good taste, which inspired me to continue."

He took a few puffs on his pipe.

"In that city, I met a distant cousin. Her name was Amelia. I thought she was the loveliest creature I had ever seen. As I said, she is the one you so remarkably resemble. She and her parents lived in San Francisco, and my parents were instrumental in making our respective presences known to the other.

"Amelia didn't especially care for the city, but she loved the ocean and the countryside. She was a free-spirit—like no woman I had ever met before. Since we were cousins, and perhaps because I was considerably older (I was 32 and Amelia a mere 18), her parents trusted us to be left alone together much more than they ever would have were I a stranger.

"I will never forget the first time I went with her to San Francisco's Ocean Beach. She took off her shoes and socks and ran barefoot along the water, jumping away from the waves, and occasionally not jumping far enough—much like a child. It may not sound like much these days, but back then women weren't supposed to show their ankles in public, let alone an entire foot."

Jennifer smiled at this and poured them both some sherry. He drank a bit before he went on.

"I was enchanted. I was certain that she was the one I had waited for my entire life." His voice turned wistful as he met her gaze. "I believe, Jennifer, that in the great scheme of the universe, there is one person above all others whose entire being is a complement to one's own. The trick is to find that other person, and once found, to recognize the quality and develop the relationship. The other person, remarkably, is often near. Since it is a planned, cosmic relationship, your paths do cross in life. But man has free-will—the source of all his joy and all his misery. How easy life would be if we just went along as victims, or guests, of our fate, no action on our part having any bearing whatsoever. I'm afraid man's destiny is not so manifest."

She nodded in response to his observations as well as his attempted humor, but she could feel the passion behind his words.

"My cousin and her parents had to go to Seattle for a business venture her father had undertaken. I was invited along. As we traveled, we passed through Brynstol. Amelia was absolutely enchanted. It was everything she had ever dreamed of as a place to live. The town was lovely, pleasant and friendly to us. The scenery was beautiful, the type of area I wanted to immortalize in my paintings. I was tired of cities also; everything that

Amelia said about the beauty of Brynstol rung equally true to my ear. I painted her portrait when we were here—just a rough sketch at the time. It wasn't until years later that I finished it in oils.

"Soon after reaching Seattle, I received a telegram that my father had died. He had been sick for a number of years, so it came as no real surprise. I knew I would be in for a sizable inheritance.

"My mother was hoping I would return east for a while to be with her until she got over the sadness of my father's death, and to take over the finances since she had no idea how to handle any of this.

"I agreed to do so, but wrote back saying that I would first need a considerable sum of money to settle my affairs in San Francisco. This was not true, but I had plans for the money.

"As I left Seattle. Amelia warmly and affectionately expressed her unhappiness at my departure, and made me promise to return to her as soon as I could. I promised, but I didn't do it, and ultimately, my delay was the cause of the disasters that happened next.

"But I was a man on a mission. With Amelia's

love filling me, on the way back to San Francisco I made a side trip to Brynstol. While here I looked at the land that was available for purchase. When I saw this hilltop I knew I had found the location that was exactly right for me...for *us*.

"I bought the land with some of the funds my mother had wired to me, and immediately— foolishly, I admit—set about finding an architect to build a house, a house which would be shared by me and my beloved Amelia.

"The closest architects I could find were in the town of Ukiah, some distance inland. We spent several weeks developing plans with many trips from Ukiah to Brynstol to make sure everything was absolutely perfect."

His voice softened as he admitted, "Those were the happiest days of my life. I wanted perfection for Amelia. I used to daydream of her reaction as she would come here and see the house. This may not seem like such an outstanding house today, but in those days it was remarkable. Amelia's house—that's how I thought of it.

"Finally I decided the architects had everything just right and I could continue with my journey. They were a competent firm, and reliable, I felt sure they would handle everything well without my constant supervision—I'm glad I was right about that at least!"

At that, his voice, his entire demeanor changed as he directly and firmly spoke, emotionless and cold. "I continued with my journey. I stopped briefly in San Francisco to take care of some finances and to give up my flat. I had other ideas about living arrangements when I returned.

"Then, I left for Boston by train.

"All in all, it had taken me quite a while to reach my mother's home, and when I arrived there I found everything to be in turmoil. In the last year of father's illness he had done very little overseeing of his business or investments, and since his death mother had done nothing at all. The way it was all going downhill she would have been destitute in six months. It was ironic that I, who never had to worry about a penny in my life, suddenly had to take charge of a family business and manipulate stocks and bonds with the motive of profit! Luckily, my schooling and its mandatory courses in economics, paid off. Also, I obviously had absorbed quite a bit more from my father than I ever would have suspected.

"It took quite a bit of work and long hours but eventually the business turned around.

"In the meantime I received progress reports from Brynstol on the house. The house was another reason I had to work so much at the business. Money that otherwise would have been profit or that I could have used to shore up inventory had to be sent to Brynstol. As each new supply of wood, rock or mortar was purchased I would receive a whopping bill. The sheer cost of delivery to the remote hilltop caused prices to skyrocket. Nevertheless, I was not being cheated. I checked and double-checked that aspect. The costs were all legitimate.

"The only gratification I received in working as diligently and single-mindedly as I did was that eventually it would pay off for Amelia and me. I wanted to get the business operating in a way that it would produce a fair profit for my mother and myself to live on. Plus all the extra thousands sent to Brynstol, I believed would be worth their weight in gold someday.

"Throughout this period I corresponded quite often with Amelia who, with her family, had returned to San Francisco. I still never told her about Brynstol. She said little about her life, and constantly ended her letters by saying that she wished I were there with her.

"Anyway, I was already over a year in Boston when my mother fell ill. I stayed several more months with her until she died. At that point I decided to sell the now flourishing business for a good profit. In all, I had been gone for more than three years. I didn't worry, though. Amelia was now twenty-one, a good age to consider marriage."

His gaze caught hers and held. She felt her breath come a little faster, a little harsher. "Once on the train to San Francisco I could hardly contain my excitement. Throughout the time in Boston, to return to Brynstol and to Amelia was like a dream, an unattainable dream of happiness. The sort of thing that happens to another man, an ordinary man perhaps, the type that marries and has a home and children, but not the sort of thing that happened to Paul Squire. Could it be that finally after so many years of feeling I was always on the outside looking in at life, that such happiness could be mine?"

His voice was hushed now. "Finally I reached San Francisco. I hurriedly checked into a hotel and sent word to Amelia that I was back and would like to see her. I went up to my hotel room to refresh myself from the journey and await her reply. The wait was agony. What if for some reason she refused to see me? What would I do? I was quite resolved I would hang myself then and there. I grew more and more impatient with each passing hour. Three times I went down to the lobby to see if the messenger boy I sent had returned with a reply and failed to bring it up to my room.

"At long last I heard a knock on the door. It was a messenger handing me the reply. You cannot imagine with what trepidation I opened that letter. It was an invitation to visit, but not in Amelia's hand.

"Confused, I hurried to the address. I was stunned when I saw it. It was a rooming house in a squalid neighborhood. Amelia's mother opened the door. I wouldn't have recognized her.

"Quickly, she explained to me that her

husband's business in Seattle had failed. In disgrace, he turned to drink and eventually left her and her daughter. They were forced to live anyway they could, often turning to begging on the streets when no other money could be found. Amelia had kept all of that a secret from me.

"A week earlier, as I was traveling, Amelia went out at night to beg for money. There was a festival near the ocean, and she went there. The rest, her mother told me, was based on conjecture and police reports…"

He stopped, finding it difficult to go on.

Jennifer reached for his hand, and placed hers atop it. Sorrowful eyes held hers a moment, then he stood and walked to the mantle, his back to her as he continued.

"Apparently, some men, drunk beyond sense, saw her and, perhaps, assumed a woman alone at night wasn't the sort of women my Amelia was. Or, they understood but didn't care. She was attacked, ravaged. The one man the police arrested said she ran from them into the ocean during the night. He claimed he tried to go after her, that he wanted to help her, that he was not a party to the attack, not one of the men who held her down…

"He said it was so dark that night, he couldn't find her in the water. He said he, himself, had gotten so turned around he found it difficult to find his way back to shore.

"Her body was found the next morning, washed up on the beach. And I knew then, if I had been there, if I had gone back to her earlier, none of that would have happened."

He stopped talking.

"I'm so sorry," Jennifer whispered.

"Her mother told me I was Amelia's hope. She said she was waiting for me, that when I arrived, everything would be all right. But I didn't, and it wasn't.

"I gave her mother money, quite a bit—the cash I carried with me for my wedding—and then I took a coach to Brynstol.

"This house, which was to be my honeymoon place, became my refuge from the world. I loved it and despised it at the same time. Daily it reminded me of Amelia and of my guilt. Loneliness became my constant companion, yet I could think of no place in the world I would rather be. But in dwelling on the 'could-have-been' I did not live the 'is.' I became sick with the obsession of my loss, and in my desire to make everything 'perfect' that I failed in my basic duty.

"I spent countless hours painting on the beach in the dampness and fog and took no care of myself. Eventually, I developed pneumonia, and with it, delirium. In that illness, the remorse I felt grew. I believed I didn't deserve what I had here—the beauty of this area, this house—and left it to return to San Francisco, getting rides along the way from people feeling sorry for the poor beggar reeling along the roadside. I had to get back to the beach in San Francisco to find—what? My lost dreams, perhaps, my hope again for life? I had this constant picture in my mind of Amelia as she was that day on the beach with me, of the two of us laughing. To laugh again, it had been years.

"I reached that beach, the place where she had laughed, and the place where she had died. I remember mothers calling their children back towards them as they saw me approach. I was searching and searching, but I never knew why. I have no idea how long I was there, all I know is that one night, there, my life ended.

"I wore no identification, and had gotten into a wretched state in my delirium. The San Francisco authorities thought they had found a dead vagrant. Very little in the way of an investigation was performed. Thus, Squire House stayed closed up for so many years, and thus was the mystery behind the strange disappearance of its even stranger owner."

Paul stopped speaking at this point and leaned back in his chair. Jennifer waited until she was sure he had come to the end of his story, then asked, "But you came back?"

He emptied out the ashes in his pipe without speaking. That having been done, he turned to Jennifer. "Yes."

"Why?"

He shook his head and then looked at the ground. "I wish I knew."

"You must have some idea," she insisted. "And what about Amelia? She never came back...or did she?"

"No. I waited for years, thinking..." He stopped talking and took a deep breath before going on. "No, she didn't return." He got up and stood in front of the fireplace. "Why should she?"

"What do you mean?"

"She had felt the joy of life. She had experienced all that was around her. Her life ended far too soon, and far too tragically, but while she was alive, she *lived.* That was why I was so attracted to her, drawn to that joy.

My life was quite the opposite. I stupidly spent it constantly looking ahead, looking at the future and ignoring the present. No one I knew satisfied me—not my parents, not my peers in school, not even the artists I met in Paris. Even—truth be told—Amelia. She was beautiful, and very kind, but I knew her only on the most superficial level. We had a few days here and there, wonderful, exciting days, and then I was gone off to take care of business.

"I made Amelia into my ideal—the perfect woman. But if I were being honest I would have to admit that, if she had lived, I don't know if we would have gotten along at all. With all that had happened, I learned from her mother that she was no longer the delicate ingénue I had met three years earlier, and I was no longer the free-spirited artist. Both of us were older, wiser, more serious, even more cynical. Of course, I never thought of any of that while I was alive. Instead, I concentrated on the love that was lost to me. I came to hate this life and all the people in it. I wanted to be alone...and alone I have been."

Jennifer was shaken by this admission, even more than hearing the tragedy of Amelia's life. His being here, his "ghostliness," he saw as punishment for having abandoned the life he was given—as if, because he had turned his back on life and wanted to be alone, he would suffer that penance throughout eternity. She pressed her hands together and lifted her fingers to her lips. "I'm sorry," she murmured.

"Don't be. It's what I wanted...or thought I wanted. And now, I've been cursed with this *aloneness*...and will be cursed with it forever."

She walked to his side and placed her hand on his arm, her heart full. "But you aren't alone any longer."

His gaze was filled with wisdom, but also detachment. A detachment that scared her. "No,

Jennifer. You must leave here. Leave me. This is my fate, not yours. I destroyed the life of one woman I loved, I won't do it to another. I want you to go."

"No!" she cried. "I don't want to leave you."

He softly touched the side of her face. "You can't stay. This is no life for a young woman."

"It can be!"

"No!" He withdrew his hand and stepped back, away from her. He held out his hand, staring at it. She did as well, and saw that it was…fading. "You see?" he said. "This corporeal me can only exist for a short time—a few hours. Then I go back to nothing, to recharge, so to speak. It's an effort." He faced her, his eyes hard, his voice harsh and raw. "It's an effort be with you! Don't you understand? I don't want you here!"

"You need me," she insisted.

"Need you? You? Surely, you're joking!"

She felt as if she'd been slapped. But she knew he didn't mean that! "Paul—"

"I want you out of this house."

"Please—"

"Have you no pride, woman?" he shouted, then

walked to the turret, arms folded and his back to her as he stared at the blackness outside. His voice colder than she had ever heard it, he said, "You're nothing to me! Nothing at all! Why would you be so stupid as to stay where you aren't wanted? How many times do I have to say it? I don't want you. I don't love you. I feel nothing for you at all."

At that, she raised her head high. "Thank you for explaining so much to me this evening."

"You asked me to," he said bitterly. "If you hadn't, I never would have bothered. Good-bye, Jennifer."

With that, he left the room.

She didn't have it in her to say anything more. He made his wishes clear. More than clear. She sat on the sofa and waited throughout the night, but he did not return.

While she was there, she was sure he never would.

There was nothing more she could do.

Chapter 23

JENNIFER PHONED BRENT the next morning. A bus would be leaving Brynstol at ten a.m. and she would be on it. When she hung up the receiver, she simply stood looking at the phone for a long time. Her heart pounded. She ached to call him back and say she made a mistake.

She wanted to stay here, but couldn't. Not after last night.

Brent was an attractive man, not a bad person. Perhaps there could be something more to their relationship.

No, who was she kidding?

Perhaps he could change, she told herself. Perhaps she could learn to love him. It was worth a try. Worth—she chuckled wryly—worth a bus ride to find out.

Whatever she did, wherever her path took her, she knew she would have to give up Squire House. Not sell it; she could never do that. But board it up, much the way Rachel had.

Paul told her he didn't want her here.

That was fine. She would go to Brent—he wanted her for the moment, at least. She was happy with this decision.

Why, then, were tears filling her eyes?

oOo

Paul Squire watched her pack.

Good riddance! I'm glad the baggage is leaving. I'll be absolutely elated to finally have my home back. Quiet, the way I like it.

No women's gaggling friends, none of her unmentionables strewn around. Make-up, perfume, hair spray. It was enough to make a ghost gag!

Thank God she rarely used any of it, except that once when she made herself up to look like Amelia...

He shut his eyes at the memory.

Foolish chit of a girl, not to know she didn't have to do that! Not to know she had grown to be so much more...

He had loved Amelia, but he had never really known her. They spent a short while together before he had to rush away. It was magical, romantic, and then tragic.

But he had gotten to know Jennifer, watching her day in and day out, with her friends, with him...

How he had enjoyed those evenings with her, talking, arguing, learning. She was a treasure to him. Remarkable in her knowledge, curiosity, enthusiasms. She seemed to understand him so well, which was astounding considering the incorporeal state he was in.

He had loved Amelia for all she might have been, but he loved Jennifer for all that she was.

I'm glad she's leaving!

Of course he was. He certainly had no need of her in his...existence...or whatever this was.

He would have thought she could have done better than Brent Cooper, however. Clearly, she didn't really care for the man.

Balderdash! He knew better than to question a woman's actions. No one could understand women, or so it was said.

And yet, he understood Jennifer...

He stiffened his spine.

Brent Cooper was a "manly" man, at least to her twenty-first century way of thinking. He had money and a good job, and she…she all but threw herself at him, the little tart! He saw her allow him to kiss her. Why, she'll probably marry him and breed a passel of ignorant brats! The two deserved each other!

Yes, he definitely was glad she was leaving.

He knew she wouldn't be back. One look all Cooper offered and she'd soon forget about him and Squire House. As far as she was concerned, he didn't exist anyway. A hallucination she had called him.

He wished it were so, because if he were nothing but a hallucination he wouldn't feel this ache deep inside; he wouldn't hear the silence of this house, or the wind weeping over its emptiness.

Or was the weeping that he heard his own?

Chapter 24

JENNIFER TOOK JOCK and Beau to Mrs. Petris' kennel. She had telephoned Mrs. Petris and explained that she was going to San Francisco for a week or so. Mrs. Petris was of course willing to keep Jock and Beau in her absence.

Jennifer hugged her dear friends goodbye almost as soon as she arrived at the Petris home. She could not bear to stay there any longer than was absolutely necessary, could not bear to answer Mrs. Petris' questions about where she was going or why. She had put leashes on the dogs so that they wouldn't try to follow her back to Squire House.

And so she handed Mrs. Petris their leads, then got on her bicycle and rode furiously back to Squire House.

There, she checked to see that everything was locked. She picked up her satchel and coat. The bus for San Francisco would be arriving in Brynstol soon. She had just enough time to make it to the bus stop. All that was left to do was to close and lock the front door—to shut that door and in so doing put an end to what had been in many ways the happiest days of her life, and also some of the saddest. At least they were certainly the most extraordinary.

She looked around the house one last time, briefly. If things worked out with Brent, the life she had here would be over. Her eye caught Paul's seascape, the first picture of his that she hung in Squire House. The picture she had selected on the day she met him. She looked at the sad blues and grays of the water—like the pale gray of his eyes. And his signature. Her eyes fixed on his signature until it completely blurred from the tears in her own eyes. Unable to bear it any longer, she hurried from the house and locked the front door behind her. She kept running to the end of her property and down the hill until she reached a point where, had she gone any further, Squire House would have been lost from view. There she stopped, and turned to look at it. It was beautiful. She stood and stared at it a while, burning every detail into her memory.

Slowly she turned and walked to the town. She

had passed along that road many times in the past, but this trip she took special care to observe the many things she had given little attention to in the past—the type of wildflower, the way the moss grew on the trees, the twists and turns in the way all the trees and vegetation grew because of the strong winds that constantly blew in from the ocean.

When Jennifer arrived in the town she stuck her head in the office of Roundmore and Innes, and brightly told them both she was going to San Francisco for a few days. Then, before they could ask a thousand and one questions, she hurried to the bus stop.

The bus was punctual, giving her little time for second thoughts about leaving, although such thoughts continually intruded. She boarded the bus and found a seat by the window on the side facing the Pacific. She watched the ocean for some time, trying to gain composure over her confused feelings. Finally, she told herself enough was enough. She was going to Brent.

Brent…she had spent so much time thinking about what she was leaving she had hardly given him any thought at all. He was personable, intelligent, handsome...also confused and troubled.

In a sense, things had come too easily for him—job, money, possessions—and he sought happiness in materialistic things. Jennifer told herself she might be the rock upon which Brent could build his life. She could show him there was more in the world than what he could buy. With a solid foundation, happiness should be attainable.

All the way to the city Jennifer tried to convince herself that she and Brent were meant for each other. It was fate. How else, after such a short acquaintance, could he profess his "almost" love? Why else, after so many months, had that "almost" love had continued? Clearly, this was the most romantic adventure she had ever known.

Slowly the bus lumbered along Highway One, down the long, twisting road that ran alongside the California coastline. Jennifer became impatient with the never ending coast, the wide Pacific, the endless water stretched out before her. More than anything else she became impatient with her own thoughts, her own doubts. She loathed having to continue with her thoughts alone, but wanted to be with someone—with Brent, who could free her mind from doubt.

Finally, in desperation, she began a conversation with the elderly woman who sat quietly beside her. The woman was going for a visit to San Francisco where she would stay with her daughter and grandchildren. Jennifer was not interested in a single word the woman said, but at least she was diverted for the remainder of the trip.

At long last the bus pulled into the downtown terminal. It was in one of the sleaziest parts of San Francisco, so she went straight to the telephone to call Brent. Under better conditions she might have decided to walk around the City a bit—she had always particularly enjoyed walking all over the North Beach-Chinatown area.

She telephoned Brent's Pacific Heights apartment. It was a very short conversation. He could hardly believe she was already there, and demanded she not move. He was coming to pick her up.

In less than fifteen minutes the familiar blue sports car turned the corner onto the street where the terminal was located. Jennifer picked up her bag and ran out to the sidewalk curb.

He leaned over and pushed the passenger door open for her. "Jenny!" he said.

She just smiled and put her suitcase in the space behind the car seats and got into the car herself. He gave her a kiss and a hug, telling her how beautiful she looked, and how happy he was to see her. She also noticed other women eying the handsome Brent and his sports car with unmasked envy.

"Have you eaten?" he asked.

"Just a candy bar from a machine in a gas station along the way. I'm not hungry, though," Jennifer replied.

"Sure you are—or will be soon," Brent answered. "I know a great little French restaurant. Do you like French food?"

"Yes, I do. But I am really tired from that long ride..." Jennifer was hoping Brent would understand that she didn't feel up to a restaurant at this point. She was hoping to move around a bit to get rid of the stiffness from the bus ride, and then to just put her feet up and relax.

"Some good food and a little wine will revive you nicely." First, he kissed her again, then smiled at her. Obviously he was a man who knew best, and he was going to take care of her. She smiled back. "Fine. Let's eat."

Brent asked how her trip was, and how the weather was in Brynstol. He told her all about the weather in San Francisco, which of course she knew already, having lived there for over thirty years.

He took her to a small but posh restaurant. Jennifer, wearing old comfortable clothes chosen for the long bus ride, felt decidedly uncomfortable. Brent, however, was obviously in his element as the maître d' called him by name, selected one of the best tables and complimented Brent on his choice of wine.

Brent ordered the dinner for the two of them. Jennifer told herself that later on, once she was not so tired and uncomfortable, she would be impressed by all this.

"Do you come here very often, Brent?" she asked.

"Fairly. It's a good place to be seen."

"You need to be seen? I hadn't realized that," she continued.

"I'm afraid television life is all about being seen."

"I should have realized..." She felt more uncomfortable than ever about her clothes.

"There are a few guys and women at the station who would cut my throat to get some of the attention I get from higher ups. It's that kind of a business." He lowered his voice to tell her that in a highly confidential manner.

"I can imagine."

He smiled. "It's worth it, though. Very lucrative, believe me."

"I do."

"This year I'm pulling in over a million bucks."

"In one year?" she gasped.

"I'll take care of you in style, Jenny." He took her hand and kissed it. "My nymph of the sea and forest."

"I know you will," she said softly.

All through dinner Brent told her about his rise up the ranks to the most popular weather reporter in San Francisco. Jennifer never before realized anyone could talk at such length about climate, money, or the accumulation of it. Up to this point her sole acquaintance with money had dealt with what to do when one didn't have enough of it.

To her surprise, she enjoyed the food very much, from the fresh salad through the veal cordon bleu to the chocolate mousse for dessert. Brent had been right that she was hungry. The only problem was that her body was so stiff from the long bus ride that she ached all over from sitting on the hard restaurant chairs.

Finally, after his third cup of coffee, Brent decided it was time for them to move on to his apartment. Jennifer was grateful.

Brent's apartment was everything she expected and more. It wasn't a rental, but his own condominium. It was on the seventeenth floor of a building high on Pacific Heights, and had a spectacular view of the northern sector of San Francisco Bay.

The hardwood floor was highly polished. The living room was decorated in shades of white, ivory and beige. It was beautiful, but Jennifer was afraid to step onto the white carpet and stood frozen by the door. As it turned out, she was glad she did because Brent offered her Japanese slippers. He explained he and his guests took their shoes off and put on slippers. In that way the guests were comfortable and his carpets and hardwood floors stayed clean and free of scuff marks. Jennifer remarked on how clever that was.

She sat on the white woolen sofa while Brent stepped behind the bar to make them each a daiquiri. The coffee table was glass with chrome around the edge and chrome legs—it looked modern and expensive. There were no paintings in the room. One wall had a chrome and wrought iron free-form sculpture, and another wall had a chrome-edged mirror. All in all the room had the appearance of being a page from an upscale magazine.

"Can I show you the rest of the house?" Brent asked.

"I would love it see it," she replied, standing.

"Right this way."

Next to the living room was a kitchen stuffed with all the latest stainless steel appliances, and granite counter tops with a bar-like eating area. Past it was a square hallway which led to the guest bathroom, the master bedroom suite, and a spare bedroom. Brent just pointed to the bathroom and spare bedroom and turned his attention to the master when Jennifer decided good manners be hanged, she wanted to see that spare bedroom that Sue had often talked about.

Saying something to the effect of, "an extra room, how nice!" she turned the knob and opened the door.

The first thought that entered Jennifer's mind when looking at that room was "Sue was right!" The room was a cornucopia of expensive toys. Brent switched on the light for Jennifer to see better.

"It is a good size room," he said, then glanced her way with a knowing smile. "Who knows? It could be a nursery one day."

In one corner of the room lay an old handbag that Jennifer recognized. It had been Sue's. A chill rippled along her back. She quickly turned off the light and shut the door, making no comment.

She turned her attention to the master bedroom. It was done in shades of beige, with starkly modern furniture. She mumbled something about "how lovely" and returned to the living room.

The daiquiri that awaited her seemed more and more appealing. She sat on the couch and took a couple of big swallows from her drink.

"How do you like the place?" Brent asked.

"It's quite nice," she said. "The view is amazing."

"Thank you. I'm glad you think so. If there's anything at all you'd like to change about it, just feel free. I know it's a man's place now, but I want you to feel comfortable here. If you want to change something, go right ahead. I'd love it if you would."

"I don't intend to live with you, Brent," Jennifer said sincerely.

"We'll see how it goes." Brent looked at her and flashed one of those heart-stopping smiles.

She had almost forgotten, in the excitement of coming to the city, of being tired, and then seeing the apartment, how handsome Brent was. She smiled back at him.

"Well, finally!" Brent said as he moved closer to her, then reached back and removed the hair clip that pulled her hair back into a twist. He ran his fingers through it, letting it fall free down her back and over her shoulders. "There, that's more like it.

Do you mind?"

"No," she said with a smile.

"I like it when you smile, although you don't do it enough," he said, then abruptly stood. "But I've got something sure to make you smile!"

She was taken aback. "You do?"

"Wait!" He opened a closet door, bent down to reach something on the floor, and came out carrying a violin case. She felt a prickling unease. "Sue told me you used to play," he said as he removed the violin and handed it to her.

Years had passed since she last held a violin in her hands. She knew the brand, not one of the very top, but more expensive than anything she had ever even touched before. Her fingers lightly ran over the warm wood, over the bow. It was beautiful.

"Sue said your playing was outstanding."

"No." Jennifer shook her head. "I wasn't. That's why I gave it up."

He handed it to her. "I know, your mother told you that you'd never be any good. She told you all kinds of things that were wrong."

Jennifer sharply faced him, stricken.

He grinned. "Who do you think Sue and I used

to talk about all year? And then, when Ross came to the city, she was forever trying to fix him up on double dates with old girl friends. I ended up talking to them, and many knew you in high school. Every last one told me the same story, that your mother dedicated herself to putting you down as a way to elevate herself. She apparently was a beauty as a young woman, voluptuous even, but as her looks left her, weight came on until she was nothing more than a woman with clothes that were too tight, makeup that was too heavy, and an even more ugly way of mocking her beautiful, talented daughter. The only one she convinced was you. They laughed, but at her, not at you."

She was stunned by this little speech. "No, that wasn't how it was."

"All of them told me the same story. You won awards for your violin playing, you could have gone on with it, but the more accolades you got, the more Rachel criticized you."

Jennifer paled at his words.

"Try it." He pointed at the violin. "For me."

It had been so long. She flexed her fingers, then tuned the instrument. It wasn't much out of tune at all, and she knew it couldn't have been sitting in the closet for very long. She played scales and a couple of exercises to warm up, surprised at how quickly the fingering came back to her after so many years.

"Play something, Jennifer," he pleaded.

"Rachel always said I was a fiddler," she told him with a grin, and launched into *Turkey in the Straw.*

She put the violin down, all but shaken by how easy it was to play it again.

"Enough with your jokes, enough with Rachel," Brent said. "Now, play the way your friends told me you could. I'd like to hear something beautiful and romantic—something that speaks to you, something you love."

One song, an aria, came immediately to mind. She used to play it all the time since she couldn't sing. She knew she would remember it; she could never forget it. "All right," she said, retuning the violin after the workout it received from her fiddling. "This is from *Madame Butterfly*. Cho-cho San sings it when she's thinking of her lover. It's in Italian, *Un Bel Di,* and she sings of how, one beautiful day, he will return…"

She began to play, and as she did, she remembered introducing the opera to Paul since it had been written after he was…gone. He had listened to it over and over, and had come to love it almost as much as she did.

She shut her eyes as she played, lost in the music. Her thoughts were filled with the words of the aria, but as the words, "*with faith, I wait for him*" came to her, she couldn't go on. She lay down the violin.

"I'm sorry," she said. "I don't remember it any longer."

"That was beautiful," he whispered.

"No, I'm rusty."

"If that's rusty, what will a little practice do for you? We'll find lessons for you. Beauty, brains, talent. I don't deserve you," he said, moving to her side.

"I'm not—"

He placed his finger over her lips, stopping her. "Don't argue. Listen to me. Believe *me.*"

"I don't—"

"Hush," he said, then kissed her, lightly at first,

then when she returned his kisses, his arms circled her and he moved ever closer as his passion grew.

She was well aware that things between them would progress this way, and progress every bit as quickly as they were. She tried to return his emotion, his passion, yet she couldn't help but remember that the last few times any man had tried to kiss her—let alone anything more—that Paul Squire had been there to interrupt. She had no need to decide whether or not she actually wanted the man's attention. Paul had settled the issue.

But now Paul Squire wasn't here. She had only herself to rely on, only herself to decide what she did, or didn't, want.

And for some reason, that seemed wrong to her. Paul Squire should be with her, but he wasn't. She felt… incomplete.

Brent leaned against her in such a way that she was pushed over onto the couch. He stretched out beside her while continuing his kisses.

Lying that way, his hands ran over her body.

Jennifer told herself she needed, wanted, a real man, a man with physical desires to match her own. And now she had one.

She opened her eyes to look at him even as his kisses continued. His eyes were shut and she couldn't help but think that he didn't look half so handsome with them shut as when they were open.

He saw her staring at him and smiled, then began unbuttoning her blouse. It was surprising how men could undo buttons with just one hand. She always used two hands herself. He got the blouse open and now was working on her bra's clasp. Jennifer smiled; his fumbling reminded her of high school.

Brent noticed her smile. Misinterpreting it, he said, "I'll get it yet," and used two hands to finally master the mysteries of a hook and eye. That done, he lowered his head and kissed her breasts.

Jennifer looked down at the top of his head, a good size head, surely with a smart, clever brain. Why, then, she wondered, did he have so little to converse about besides himself? It seemed such a waste. Paul, on the other hand, had a slender, fine-boned build, yet every microbe of his being was filled with knowledge. She was glad that great store of knowledge hadn't been lost when death came to him. What a tragedy that would have been. And the miraculous thing was that she learned from him a little bit about how mysterious and yet wonderful, in the true sense of the word, this life could be.

But she had given all that up. And why shouldn't she? She had Brent now, and they would belong to each other completely in a short time the way things were progressing. That was what she wanted, she reminded herself. Wasn't it? He was starting to play in the area of her thighs now.

She shut her eyes, trying to block all thought, trying to allow herself to simply feel.

But her mind wouldn't stop. She hadn't really given Paul up, he gave her up. He ordered her to leave. How could he be so cruel?

"Sorry," Brent said, bringing Jennifer out of her reverie. He had unzipped her slacks and now had to lift her behind a bit off the sofa in order to slide them off of her.

"Oh sure," she said, and helped him. That taken care of, Brent continued where he had left off. He was skilled and knew where and how to touch her to awaken her senses.

Yet, her mind, her wayward mind, would not shut down. Paul's actions had definitely been cruel, she thought. He never should have left her that way. She had done nothing to upset him. Why didn't he see that? Why could he not recognize such a simple fact? She had tried so many times to talk to him—but got nowhere. None of this with Brent would have happened if he hadn't turned away from her. It was his fault!

She had to find love where she might, and now she had succeeded. Her arms tightened around Brent and she kissed him back, trying to find the passion that had been so lacking in her life.

What Paul did to her was the same as he had done to Amelia. He left Amelia, and by the time he returned, it was too late. She wondered if Amelia, too, had felt abandoned.

But Amelia hadn't felt abandoned. She waited for him, and Paul did return.

Amelia had waited....

The thought swirled around Jennifer's mind time and again.

Paul had said to her, *"I destroyed the life of one woman I loved, I won't do it to another."*

Another...He did love her, but he feared for her if she stayed with him.

"This is no life for a young woman like you," he had added.

She understood, then, why he told her to leave. He was afraid of his feelings for her, afraid of the life she would lead if she stayed with him. But it wasn't his choice, it was hers. Just as Amelia's choices, and the consequences of them, weren't his fault no matter how much guilt he chose to take on.

He was at Squire House, choosing to wait alone for eternity. *There is one person above all others whose entire being is a complement to one's own,* he had told her, and the hardest part was to recognize that, to find that love and to hold onto it.

Could that be why, no matter how hard she looked, she could never find the "right" man until Paul?

She bolted upright on the couch.

Brent looked at her in surprise, "What?" was all he could say.

"It would be much more comfortable in your bedroom," she said. "Why don't you go ahead? Give me a moment and then I'll join you. Okay?" She smiled at him.

Brent winked as he said "Great!" He leapt off

the couch and strutted to his bedroom.

Jennifer immediately put her slacks back on, buttoned and adjusted her clothing, picked up her bags, slipped on her shoes and took a step towards the door. She glanced back at the violin. Brent had given it to her, but she couldn't take it. She couldn't take anything from him.

Maybe someday soon, she'd buy one for herself—one she could afford. In fact, she knew she would.

That decided, she quietly crept out the door. She pushed the button for the elevator, and the longest twenty seconds in her life were spent waiting for that elevator to arrive.

Once on the street she headed towards Van Ness Avenue, a main thoroughfare. She had gone no more than half a block when a taxi turned onto the street. She hailed it and told the driver she wanted the downtown bus terminal. As the taxi started off she leaned back on the car seat and let out a sigh of relief. She felt good for the first time since yesterday.

In a short while they were at the bus station. Jennifer decided to look for any bus heading north.

She didn't want to stay at the station on the off chance that Brent might come looking for her demanding an explanation.

There was an all-night express to Portland that made one stop in Eureka. It would take her about two hours farther north than she needed to go, but somehow that seemed preferable to waiting in the station for the morning bus to Brynstol.

After only an hour's wait the bus was ready to roll. Soon, it had crossed the Golden Gate Bridge, leaving San Francisco behind and heading for the rugged northern counties. Jennifer had chosen this way of life once before, over a year ago, almost as a whim. She knew this time what she was doing, and she felt at peace.

Only once did she wonder what Brent thought as he waited in his bedroom, finally to go out to the living room to discover that she had gone. She wondered if, deep down, he hadn't felt relieved. She knew she would never see him again.

The bus moved briskly in the still darkness of the night.

Only an occasional neon sign along the highway let her know there was life outside the perimeters of the bus. She soon fell into an uneasy asleep.

The lack of motion as the bus came to a stop must have been what caused her to wake up, for the bus driver was careful to cause no lurch or jolt to his sleeping passengers. Nevertheless, most of them did awaken.

"Eureka," the driver said as he opened the door and stood to help any of his passengers that might need assistance.

She picked up her bag and got off the bus. She went into the station to see when she could get a ride to Brynstol. The bus southbound would leave Eureka at 8 a.m., and reach Brynstol at 10:30. It was just 10:30 yesterday that she had left Brynstol for San Francisco.

As it was currently a little before 6 a.m., she had two hours to wait. She bought a newspaper and went to a small cafe in the station for coffee and doughnuts. She found that despite how early it was, she felt surprisingly well rested. Just four and a half hours more and she would be home again. She could hardly wait.

Paul would know she was back. She was sure

of that, and someday he would return to her. She decided that she should figure out some way to cause him to come back even sooner than he might otherwise. Perhaps if she threatened to slash one of his paintings? Or to burn down Squire House? Or worse, turn it into a bed and breakfast?

No, he would know she could never go through with any of that. He knew she loved the house and land almost as much as he did.

Still, what if he never returned? Could that happen? Jennifer knew it was possible. Would he do such a thing? If so, she would wait for him there—until her own eternity if need be.

Finally eight o'clock arrived and Jennifer boarded what she hoped would be the last bus she would ever have to ride in her life.

On the bus Jennifer realized that the most difficult thing about the life she chose would be dealing with friends. She knew Sue, for one, would immediately begin a campaign to match her with some fellow. Jennifer shrugged. There were worse crosses to bear.

The two and one-half hour bus ride seemed interminably long.

She grew increasingly impatient whenever the bus pulled into some little town where no one got on or off.

All that Jennifer could think of was to get back to Squire House as quickly as possible. She longed to see the familiar house once again.

Finally the bus turned off of Highway One onto Brynstol's Main Street. The familiar shops came into view. The bus slowed then stopped in front of the familiar little bench that served as Brynstol's "bus station," and Jennifer jumped off. She decided that she would not even stop to see Mr. Innes—she didn't want to have to make up any stories yet about her day in San Francisco, nor did she want to explain why she was on the bus heading south from Eureka instead of north from the city. All she wanted to do was to go home. Later she would bicycle to Mrs. Petris' place to pick up her dogs, then say hello to Innes. But not yet.

She saw a couple of people she knew on the road to her house. She waved at them in passing and kept on going. It was a cold, brisk morning, heavy with fog, but no rain. To Jennifer, the weather was beautiful.

She made her way up the winding road as quickly as she could. She was slightly out of breath as she reached the last bend, when Squire House appeared ahead of her. All her energy rushed back as she viewed the house, a little foreboding, a little sad, and a whole lot wonderful. She slowly walked the rest of the way, no longer wanting to rush, but simply to enjoy every nuance of light and color and scenery.

How familiar yet how novel it all looked. The hillside, the sounds of the omnipresent gulls with their squawks and shrills of fights and bragging of fine catches, the smells of the ocean and the pines.

She reached the door to the house and took the key out of her handbag. It seemed strange to use a key to enter.

She put the key in the lock and turned it. Home at last! Jennifer stepped inside, put down her bags and stood still, enjoying the feel of the house, the air, the scent…

Jennifer's heart thudded with hope as she hesitantly moved towards the living room. The familiar aroma of pipe tobacco became ever stronger. Could it be? Dare she hope? She heard no sound. She took one step then another, another, until she was in the living room, her eyes riveted towards the leather chair. Empty! But then, disappointment weighing on every fiber, she glanced around the room and saw him standing silently before the windows in the turret watching her. Their eyes locked.

"Paul," she whispered.

"You came back." His voice was cold as it had been the last time they met, yet she saw a spark of something in them—warmth? hope?—that he could not mask.

"I did. I had to." She took several steps towards him, but stopped, unsure.

"Had to?" He lifted his chin.

She turned her head; it was easier not to look at him, but then she knew she had to reveal herself, to be truthful…and to hope.

She forced her eyes to meet his. "I love you," she said simply. He looked stricken, as if he could not believe what he had heard. "I love you and after a long search, I found you. I don't know why or how—perhaps you've been waiting for me, or perhaps we missed each other in your life. Who knows? But you're here now because you love me too, no matter how much you rage and bluster and do all you can to deny it." She fought the tears that threatened; she would not cry. "Your life was empty, as mine is without you; as mine has always been without you."

She looked up at him with pleading and longing, praying his former resolutions would melt. When he said nothing, she continued. "Can we be given another chance, Paul? Can love fill lives that have been mere shadows of existence up to now? Is that what this is about?"

He shut his eyes a moment. "I wish I knew what was best," he whispered, then smiled wryly at himself. "I thought it would be fun, at first, to have someone to talk to now and then. But as I got to know you, you stole my heart. It was wrong. I soon realized that. I stayed away for your sake, hoping you would want to leave here." He shook his head at the memory. "How it hurt to see you unhappy, to see you alone. Last Christmas I could barely stand it. But if I saw you again, I feared my resolve would be lost for love of you, and you would no longer have your choice."

She was heart-sick by his words, but she understood what he meant. "My choice, yes, I had a choice. You did give me that. And now I know for sure this is what I want. This is my life, and I'll live it fully with you. Perhaps, in some small way, that will help make up for all you lost so long ago."

He gave her a small smile. "Lost? I haven't lost anything. You are more than I could have dreamed." His expression turned serious then, and more intense than she had ever seen it. "I've come to love you this past year, and who knows how long before that? And I will for all eternity."

"For all eternity," she repeated, then reached out her hand to him. He took it and raised it to his lips in a kiss, a strange, ethereal kiss. But it was enough, definitely enough.

Her heart filled with love for this man, more than she had ever known possible. He lit a warming fire, then sat by her side on the sofa, his arm around her, and her head resting on his shoulder.

Squire House stood like a fortress on the hilltop by the sea, braving the fog-laden air of wind-swept vistas, as it had for over a century, and as it would for many years to come.

About the Author

Joanne Pence was born and raised in northern California. She has been an award-winning, *USA Today* best-selling author of mysteries for many years, but she has also written historical fiction, contemporary romance, romantic suspense, a fantasy, and supernatural suspense. All of her books are now available as ebooks, and most are also in print. Joanne hopes you'll enjoy her books, which present a variety of times, places, and reading experiences, from mysterious to thrilling, emotional to lightly humorous, as well as powerful tales of times long past.

Visit her at www.joannepence.com and be sure to sign up for Joanne's mailing list to hear about new books.

The Rebecca Mayfield Mysteries

Rebecca is a by-the-book detective, who walks the straight and narrow in her work, and in her life. Richie, on the other hand, is not at all by-the-book. But opposites can and do attract, and there are few

316 | Joanne Pence

mystery two-somes quite as opposite as Rebecca and Richie.

ONE O'CLOCK HUSTLE – North American Book Award winner in Mystery

TWO O'CLOCK HEIST

THREE O'CLOCK SÉANCE

FOUR O'CLOCK SIZZLE

FIVE O'CLOCK TWIST

SIX O'CLOCK SILENCE

Plus a Christmas Novella: The Thirteenth Santa

The Angie & Friends Food & Spirits Mysteries

Angie Amalfi and Homicide Inspector Paavo Smith are soon to be married in this latest mystery series. Crime and calories plus a new "twist" in Angie's life in the form of a ghostly family inhabiting the house she and Paavo buy, create a mystery series with a "spirited" sense of fun and adventure.

COOKING SPIRITS

ADD A PINCH OF MURDER

COOK'S BIG DAY

MURDER BY DEVIL'S FOOD

Plus a Christmas mystery-fantasy: COOK'S CURIOUS CHRISTMAS

And a cookbook: COOK'S DESSERT COOKBOOK

The early "Angie Amalfi mystery series" began when Angie first met San Francisco Homicide Inspector Paavo Smith. Here are those mysteries in the order written:

SOMETHING'S COOKING

TOO MANY COOKS

COOKING UP TROUBLE

COOKING MOST DEADLY

COOK'S NIGHT OUT

COOKS OVERBOARD

A COOK IN TIME

TO CATCH A COOK

BELL, COOK, AND CANDLE

IF COOKS COULD KILL

TWO COOKS A-KILLING

COURTING DISASTER

RED HOT MURDER

THE DA VINCI COOK

Supernatural Suspense

Ancient Echoes

Top Idaho Fiction Book Award Winner

Over two hundred years ago, a covert expedition shadowing Lewis and Clark disappeared in the wilderness of Central Idaho. Now, seven anthropology students and their professor vanish in the same area. The key to finding them lies in an ancient secret, one that men throughout history have sought to unveil.

Michael Rempart is a brilliant archeologist with a colorful and controversial career, but he is plagued by a sense of the supernatural and a spiritual intuitiveness. Joining Michael are a CIA consultant on paranormal phenomena, a washed-up local sheriff, and a former scholar of Egyptology. All must overcome their personal demons as they attempt to save the students and learn the expedition's terrible secret....

Ancient Shadows

One by one, a horror film director, a judge, and a newspaper publisher meet brutal deaths. A link exists between them, and the deaths have only begun ....

Archeologist Michael Rempart finds himself pitted against ancient demons and modern conspirators when a dying priest gives him a powerful artifact—a pearl said to have granted Genghis Khan the power, eight centuries ago, to lead his Mongol warriors across the steppes to the gates of Vienna.

The artifact has set off centuries of war and destruction as it conjures demons to play upon men's strongest ambitions and cruelest desires. Michael realizes the so-called pearl is a philosopher's stone, the prime agent of alchemy. As much as he would like to ignore the artifact, when he sees horrific deaths and experiences, first-hand, diabolical possession and affliction, he has no choice but to act, to follow a path along the Old Silk Road to a land that time forgot, and to somehow find a place that may no longer exist in the world as he knows it.

Historical, Contemporary & Fantasy Romance

Dance with a Gunfighter

Gabriella Devere wants vengeance. She grows up quickly when she witnesses the murder of her family by a gang of outlaws, and vows to make them pay for their crime. When the law won't help her, she takes matters into her own hands.

Jess McLowry left his war-torn Southern home to head West, where he hired out his gun. When he learns what happened to Gabriella's family, and what she plans, he knows a young woman like her will have no chance against the outlaws, and vows to save her the way he couldn't save his own family.

But the price of vengeance is high and Gabriella's willingness to sacrifice everything ultimately leads to the book's deadly and startling conclusion.

Willa Cather Literary Award finalist for Best Historical Novel.

The Dragon's Lady

Turn-of-the-century San Francisco comes to life in this romance of star-crossed lovers whose love is forbidden by both society and the laws of the time.

Ruth Greer, wealthy daughter of a shipping magnate, finds a young boy who has run away from his home in Chinatown—an area of gambling parlors, opium dens, and sing-song girls, as well as families trying to eke out a living. It is also home to the infamous and deadly "hatchet men" of Chinese lore.

There, Ruth meets Li Han-lin, a handsome, enigmatic leader of one such tong, and discovers he is neither as frightening cruel, or wanton as reputation would have her believe. As Ruth's fascination with the lawless area grows, she finds herself pulled deeper into its intrigue and dangers, particularly those surrounding Han-lin. But the two are from completely different worlds, and when both worlds are shattered by the Great Earthquake and Fire of 1906 that destroyed most of San Francisco, they face their ultimate test.

Seems Like Old Times

When Lee Reynolds, nationally known television news anchor, returns to the small town where she was born to sell her now-vacant childhood home, little does she expect to find that her first love has moved back to town. Nor does she expect that her feelings for him are still so strong.

Tony Santos had been a major league baseball player, but now finds his days of glory gone. He's gone back home to raise his young son as a single dad.

Both Tony and Lee have changed a lot. Yet, being with him, she finds that in her heart, it seems like old times...

The Ghost of Squire House

For decades, the home built by reclusive artist, Paul Squire, has stood empty on a windswept cliff overlooking the ocean. Those who attempted to live in the home soon fled in terror. Jennifer Barrett knows nothing of the history of the house she inherited. All she knows is she's glad for the chance to make a new life for herself.

It's Paul Squire's duty to rid his home of intruders, but something about this latest newcomer's vulnerable status ... and resemblance of someone from his past ... dulls his resolve. Jennifer would like to find a real flesh-and-blood man to liven her days and nights—someone to share her life with—but living in the artist's house, studying his paintings, she is surprised at how close she feels to him.

A compelling, prickly ghost with a tortured, guilt-ridden past, and a lonely heroine determined to start fresh, find themselves in a battle of wills and emotion in this ghostly fantasy of love, time, and chance.

Dangerous Journey

C.J. Perkins is trying to find her brother who went missing while on a Peace Corps assignment in Asia. All she knows is that the disappearance has something to do with a "White Dragon." Darius Kane, adventurer and bounty hunter, seems to be her only hope, and she practically shanghais him into helping her.

With a touch of the romantic adventure film Romancing the Stone, C.J. and Darius follow a trail that takes them through the narrow streets of Hong Kong, the backrooms of San Francisco's Chinatown, and the wild jungles of Borneo as they pursue both her brother and the White Dragon. The closer C.J. gets to them, the more danger she finds herself in—and it's not just danger of losing her life, but also of losing her heart.

Made in the USA
Coppell, TX
15 November 2020